Minstrel of a Modern Time

**By
David Telford**

Airleaf
Publishing

airleaf.com

© Copyright 2005, David Telford

All Rights Reserved.

No part of this book may be reproduced, stored in a retrieval system, or transmitted by any means, electronic, mechanical, photocopying, recording, or otherwise, without written permission from the author.

ISBN: 1-59453-766-6

Acknowledgements

The first thing you are told when you ask for advice on writing a book is "write what you know." That being the case, I was hard pressed to decide what it is exactly that I know. I know a little bit about a lot of things but I don't know a lot about much. This left me with very few literary genres with which to work.

I do know about *me*. I know about *my world*. I know about the people I come into contact with at least to the degree that we interact. I know about love. I know about desire – specifically the desire to reach beyond what I know, and experience more than what is reachable within my four walls. These concepts were the motivation for this story and I have a lot of people to thank for this.

First and foremost I need to thank my grandmother, Ada, for lessons in love. She came into our family when my grandfather remarried and long after we had established our familial relationships. She took us all as her own and has never thought of us as anything but *her* kids. That immediate selfless love is a key theme in this story.

I have to thank my father for the desire to reach out into the world. I'm not sure if wanderlust is genetic or environmental but either way I was born with a need to see other places and experience other people. This requires the acceptance of risk when meeting new people or entering strange lands as you never know who you'll meet or what adventures will befall you once you take that first step. This too is a foundational element in this story.

Thanks go to my mother and many of my ancestors along her line for the need to express myself creatively. Much of their imaginative nature is captured in the characters within, and without it pumping through my own veins, I might never have written anything.

Finally, thanks go to the people I've met on my own journeys for lending their personalities, trivialities, and sometimes names to this story. You know who you are. Your contributions to my story are reflected in these pages. Thanks to all.

January 31, 2004
Aurora, IL

In our lives, the path we take
Is of our own election
But when two paths like ours converge
They take a new direction.

And though we may find miles of woe
Or shallow trails of tears,
I'll walk those miles with you my love,
Throughout the coming years.

As hand in hand we walk this road
Our footsteps will fall true.
For, ever shall you walk with me,
And I will walk with you.

- Angus Tory McLeod

Beginning
A Place to Start

There was a time when going out to the mailbox was one of the highlights of my day. Back when I was writing for a variety of magazines and papers I received a large number of packages with return addresses for *Time Magazine*, *The Atlantic Monthly*, *The Saturday Evening Post*, *New England Times*, and even *Rolling Stone*. It wasn't difficult to be the talk of the town in Mertztown, Pennsylvania. There wasn't a hell of a lot of anything else to talk about. So, I became a local celebrity and although it meant I couldn't go into the hardware store without hearing the hushed gossip of what *that McCormick fella was workin' on*, I didn't mind.

I retired from the wordsmith business a few years back. Oh, I still pen a sporadic poem now and then and have two or three unpublished short stories sitting in my files. But my commercial work is done. Instead, I spend my time tinkering around the house, painting or sketching down by the creek, and now and then sneaking up on my wife MaryBeth to give her a bear hug or a pinch on her broadening bottom. It's a simple life, far removed from the excitement of deadlines, contracts, and debating editors, but it's nice in its own bucolic sort of way.

MaryBeth was born for her rustic life. She buys and refinishes antiques, cans pickles, beets, tomatoes, and whatever else we happen to find in our haphazard garden, and takes long walks with Morton our German shepherd out along the creek. A few years back I took a stab at photography and actually captured a wonderful shot of her pumping through the hills, swinging her long walking stick like a land-locked oarsman. We have that one framed and mounted over the fireplace opposite a more professional shot of our only daughter, Jenna. And since this story is more about Jenna than my wife, my dog, or me, I'll forego any further self-indulgence and focus on the task at hand.

Growing up, we knew Jenna was going to be a traveler. Even as a toddler she had a tendency to wander away from us the moment we turned our backs. She was always trying to find out what was around the next corner, or behind the next door. And she never had trouble talking to strangers, which only increased our anxiety during her formative years. But as she grew, she became a constant source of joy in our lives – always laughing or making us laugh.

Two days before her seventeenth birthday things changed.

Jenna had just jumped off the school bus that dropped her in front of our long driveway. As she was crossing the street in front of the bus a car struck her. The driver had dropped something on the floor of his car and as he reached to pick up whatever it was, he swerved into the left-hand lane, just missing a rear-end collision with the bus itself. When he looked up it was too late, he was already past the bus and Jenna was already in his path.

She spent three weeks in the hospital while her

broken legs, pelvis, and shoulder healed. She also had a significant concussion and had lost a fair amount of blood due to some internal injuries. Surgery fixed the internal damage, the concussion faded, and her youthful regenerative skills healed the broken bones. The doctor assured us she would be able to walk properly once she was healed. In fact, she told us that Jenna would be 100% within the year. That turned out to be mostly true.

We had heard about HIV and AIDS through the media so we knew that these acronyms were bad news. In 1987, however, it was still considered a disease known only to drug users and homosexuals. Those of us outside of those lifestyles felt safe. What we didn't expect was that the nation's blood supply could be contaminated. It wasn't until Jenna fought a particularly stubborn cold that turned into pneumonia that we found out just how unsafe we really were. She had contracted HIV from a transfusion she was given after her accident.

Being a writer, research came easy to me and in no time I was up to speed on the nature of the virus and Acquired Immune Deficiency Syndrome and could probably talk as intelligently about it as the experts on television. Jenna also did her homework and in true Jenna-fashion determined that her condition would never degrade into full-blown AIDS. She just wouldn't let it. She had too much to do in her life and couldn't be bothered to let that happen. I'll tell you what, her conviction was contagious and she almost had me convinced as well!

Things continued on for a while as if all were well. Even though everything seemed normal, I know that at least in the back of my mind those dreaded acronyms kept stirring up trouble. MaryBeth was not as good at hiding her feelings and would often come back from her long walks red-faced and puffy-eyed. Despite this she never once brought up the subject. She dealt with it privately.

Then, on the anniversary of the car accident that initiated this new phase of our lives, two days before her twenty-first birthday, Jenna woke up, packed a backpack with clothes, some food, and a little cash, and disappeared. She left quietly before either MaryBeth or I had wakened. If she had been planning this for some time, we were unaware. We simply woke up to find a note on the mirror of MaryBeth's bureau.

November 9, 1992
Dearest Folks –

I've given this a lot of thought. I need to get away for a while, maybe for more than a while. So much has changed since the accident – four years ago today! You guys did everything you could to make me believe that things would be the same and that this evil little bug wasn't moving around inside me waiting to detonate. I love you for that and for everything you've done and meant to me.

I need to find something and I don't even know what it is. I do know that I'm not going to find it at home. I feel like there's some great white whale waiting for me out in the world and I have to find it while I still have the opportunity. I may never actually find what I'm looking for but I know if I don't try then I'll find myself wasting away on a hospital bed someday wishing I had.

I promise to write and tell you how I'm doing and where I've been. It doesn't do much good to have an adventure if you can't share it with someone! Don't worry! I'll be smart. I'll be safe. I'll write soon.

I love you,
Jenna

David Telford

    P.S. Daddy, I took $30 from your wallet. Thanks.
    P.P.S. I fed Morton before I left.
    P.P.P.S. Morton peed a little on the kitchen floor. I cleaned it up.

Continuation
On the Road

When Jenna was on the road, living out her days in pursuit of her white whale, she wrote to us regularly. The mailbox became our only source of contact with her but unfortunately the communication was one way. At least once each week, sometimes twice, we would receive a letter-sized envelope stuffed with pages covered with Jenna's curly script, margins and all, detailing the latest leg of her quest and her revelations about life in general. After a while, despite our concern for how well she was eating, where she was sleeping, and the progress of her disease, MaryBeth and I would feel a rush of excitement when Tipper Galloway pulled up in his US Mail Jeep.

Our Jenna, our daughter, our only child, was on an adventure that we would never have even dreamed of undertaking ourselves.

The last letter we received from her was in late May of 1993.

There was nothing special about the letter, simply a hurried collection of thoughts and experiences, scratched across every possible inch of lined paper and numbered not by page, but by story or concept. She gave us no word of her condition or any reason to be any more concerned than usual so we simply enjoyed her letter and waited eagerly for the next one.

But the next letter never came and the weeks that followed wore heavily on us, as we were certain that her disease had taken her on some back road, far from help of any kind. Our worries proved to be only partially confirmed as later in June we received a letter from a hospital in Stockton, California informing us that Jenna had died while under their care. I flew out to California and arranged to have her body flown home. We buried her ashes out along the fence and put up a marker.

We visit that spot daily.

From that point on the mailbox was not so dear a companion as it had once been. Only the steady flow of bills, magazines, and junk mail made the long trip up the hill in Tipper's Jeep. Then one day we received a strange package. In it we found a sketch of our daughter, a cassette tape, a letter from Jenna that had never been mailed, and a spiral notebook containing a long letter from a man claiming to be Jenna's husband.

**March 11, 1994 – Chicago, IL
Dear Mom and Dad,**

 I know it must seem odd to receive a letter from a stranger with the above salutation. The truth is that I've been hesitant to write you at all. But fate and a nagging conscience put this notebook on my lap and this pen in my hand, so I thought I had better make the best of it and let the consequences have at me in the end.
 I knew your daughter, Jenna. I was with her when she died. I found the enclosed letter in her things. I apologize for not sending it sooner but I think that now is as good a time as any, all things considered.
 I guess I should let you know who I am and why I'm writing.
 My name is Angus Tory McLeod and I am Jenna's husband – your son-in-law. I know that may come as a shock. She really did want to tell you about me, as is evident in the enclosed letter. I'm not sure why she never sent it and perhaps it was because she never sent it that I've been so hesitant to write to you myself. At first, I thought she might not want you to know about me, about our marriage, about the life we shared for the brief time we were together. After all, I'm not the type of man that parents hope their daughters will fall in love with. But the more I thought about it, the more important it

became that I contact you. You see, I was with her in the end and I think that it's your right as her parents to know how she spent the last few weeks of her life – to know that she was happy and that she thought of you often. Once that revelation made itself clear to me, I found myself with a notebook and pen and the words, I hope, to describe what we experienced together.

I suppose I should start with an introduction.

A lot of different words can be used to describe me – traveler, vagabond, vagrant, and others. I suppose I could even be called a gypsy of sorts. I prefer to think of myself more in romantic terms – a spiritual nomad, if you will. But regardless of the brand I carry, I am a homeless wanderer, living my life day-by-day, meal-by-meal. My possessions are few and I carry them all with me. I won't go into a lengthy inventory as it will serve no purpose, so I'll defer.

I have been on the road since my parents died six years ago. My family is extremely small so other than an aunt who is a borderline sociopath, I had no one to turn to. With no property to speak of and no room in an orphanage for a nineteen year old, I was left to drift in the world; out on my own, as it were.

At first I loved the freedom of the road. It was scary enough, scavenging a meal or a warm, dry bed, but at nineteen, there was a certain thrill to that "skin-of-the-teeth" existence. After a while, however, the novelty wore off and I found myself in a true life-or-death struggle on a daily basis. The stress of survival often brought with it depression and hopelessness.

I can't stand the nights in homeless shelters watching

people collect in a room, most of them seeming to simply put in time, waiting for death to eventually come along. A few nights of listening to the non-stop shouting and banshee-like cry of the sick and deranged, and I had my fill of that facet of the American Dream.

By my twentieth birthday I had become a veteran road warrior, traveling the secondary highways from city to city, sleeping under trees and bridges, working for meals as often as I could. Now and then I'd grab a ride with a friendly trucker, most of them looking for someone to keep them awake during the long all-nighters. Some were hoping for a different sort of company. Fortunately I am endowed with the ability to be gracious yet unyielding in those situations. Although it often meant that my ride was cut short, I was never forced into a compromising position and often left with a handshake, warm wishes, and a few bucks to get myself a meal.

As part of my modest collection of belongings I have an old, but trusty acoustic guitar. The frets are worn and the E-string tends to fall out of tune more often than I like, but this devoted friend has helped me to secure many a meal in towns where my kind are not always welcome. I call my guitar "Erik" after the pitiful creature that haunted the Paris Opera house in Leroux's *Phantom of the Opera*. He's not much to look at but his voice is his beauty. I carved his name into his neck. Upon reflection I realized what a horrid thing that was to do to such a loyal friend. Still, Erik bares his name proudly – gouged into his chipped, lacquered surface.

I don't want you to think that I have been nothing but

a derelict scavenging off the good will of hard working people. In the time that I have been traveling, I have made an effort to keep current on world events and have taken a voracious liking to the study of philosophy. I satisfy my hunger in libraries across the country, sometimes spending several hours at a stretch, pouring over the collections of classical and even satirical authors. My own personal philosophy, erected despite, and in some small part, in spite of the teachings of those before me, can be effectively distilled down to two words: *Carpe Diem*.

I know, sir, that you're a writer so I won't insult you with the translation. Although looking back now, at the previous sentence, I see that it might have been quicker to do just that rather than present a lengthy explanation as to why I wouldn't, and then follow it up with a lengthy description of that realization. Ah, if only I had a pencil with a good sturdy eraser!

I carved those two words into Erik's neck as well, but I don't think he minded as much when I did that, as I had not yet named him. I think that once you give something a name, you owe it a little more respect than when it was just a thing. That being the case, I won't be carving into Erik again.

But to return to my previous topic, I have learned that while most people will freely give to a person in need, it is often far more meaningful if one can return something to them in lieu of payment. For this reason I carry a notebook and a sketchpad with me. I return the kindness of my benefactors with a song, a poem, or more often, a sketch of their house, or their dog, or themselves

– something to let them know that I do not see them as a faceless handout. I want them to see the same beauty in themselves and their world that I see in their kindness and charity. I know that telling you this may seem self-serving, and perhaps it is, but it's important to me for you to know that the stigma of the freeloader is something I work hard to avoid. I have no money so I try to return a little beauty. I like to think that my effort is successful.

So, I have traveled the country. I have been in New York, Chicago, Los Angeles, Dallas, Seattle, Miami and a dozen other major cities, as well as the lesser known towns of Horseheads, NY, Church Hill, TN, Lapeer, MI, Burlington, IA and the like. Of course there have been smaller towns, some with no more than two or three hundred inhabitants, but all with their own particular charm and beauty. I even saw a sign for Mertztown while crossing through the glorious hills of eastern PA, but that was long before I met Jenna and was not aware at the time of any sort of karmic link to your town. I recall wondering at the time if everyone in Mertztown was named Fred and Ethel, like from the old Lucy show. I thought Jenna would laugh herself unconscious the first time I brought that up.

I have met a great many people on the road. Some are wanderers like me but mostly regular folks with jobs and families and mortgages. The best people I found were those from the small, isolated villages that scatter the wide-open areas of the Midwest. Many of these people close their minds to the world beyond their town borders, but they are gracious and charitable and have provided me with more than my share of memorable stories.

There are those, however, who do not know tolerance as their personal savior. I have been beaten several times by a variety of locals, and on occasion been locked up in small-town jails for the standard 21 days for vagrancy. These stints behind bars are not so terrible, especially after a long stretch of road when the rain just won't stop and your stomach bellows in protest of its emptiness. In jail the food is hot, the beds are warm and dry, the showers wash the road off, and they provide medicine if you're sick. After three weeks of this high life, I'm back on the road feeling much better for the experience. Sometimes they even provide a bus ticket to the next large city to make sure you actually leave. I always try to be cooperative with the local authorities. I punctuate my answers with all the proper titles; sir, officer, and your honor. I know that the way I live is shunned in these towns and I mark them off on my faded road atlas as places to avoid.

Despite my appreciation for the amenities of America's concrete hotels, I prefer to work for my meals. Erik and I frequently perform at bars and truck stops along the way. The owners of these establishments usually provide a meal, sometimes a warm room to curl up in for the night, and every now and then a few dollars to get me to the next "gig."

My repertoire of songs includes some of the less raucous pop tunes, a few Country and Western numbers and an occasional ballad in the style of Woody Guthrie or Pete Seeger – two men who I consider the greatest of modern-day minstrels. I also have a dozen or so original tunes that I slip into a set. The enclosed cassette tape contains a less than professional rendition of the last song I wrote – *Three Weeks in June*. I wrote this song in the hospital while Jenna slept. I sang it for her only twice. This tape is a recording of the third time I performed it. Probably the last.

I suppose I should stop rattling on about myself and tell you about Jenna – how we met, the progression of our relationship, our marriage, and the final days in California. I think that may have to wait until tomorrow as there's a large policeman looking at me and I suspect he'll be directing me to leave the park any minute now as it's getting quite late. Best to beat him to the punch I think.

David Telford

March 12 – Still in Chicago

I read through the start of this letter and was more than once tempted to rip out those pages and start over. However, I want this to be an honest letter so I think my first draft should also be my final draft. I hope I manage to come across as I intend. But enough self-analysis!

I had been walking for three days north on Route Whatever toward, through, and out of Wichita, KS. Some unseen cosmic force must have been in effect as I could not catch a ride from of any of the passing cars or trucks. Perhaps my hitching thumb was cold. Perhaps I looked a bit more bedraggled due to the wind and rain and thereby less trustworthy than usual. But regardless of the reason I put the miles on breaking only for a few hours of sleep at a time.

I tried my best to locate an opportunity for a meal in exchange for work but nobody seemed to have anything that needed doing. I found that strange, particularly in late May when everybody who has a yard has yard work. Still, who knows what fuel is used in the machinery that drives us toward our fate? Had I been able to procure a meal or two, I would not have been as desperately hungry by the third day of my long walk, and I may have strolled on by the truck stop where *she* sat waiting on the porch.

Barb O's is the classic greasy spoon where long haul truckers stop for a well-needed dose of caffeine and cholesterol. The eggs are under done, the sausage and potatoes drip with grease, and the coffee is blacker than a cave and thick enough to float a sugar cube. God bless America!

My stomach was performing an opera in five parts by the time I stumbled up Barb O's wooden steps. The parking lot was relatively empty with only a scattering of eighteen-wheelers and one or two pick-ups, probably belonging to local fans of Barb O's menu. The lack of business was a bit disconcerting to me as I would be more likely to arrange a meal-for-work trade if they were moderately busy and needed a fair amount of dishes washed.

Still, my angry stomach and cramping bowels pressed me on in hopes that a charitable soul was in charge that day.

As I walked up the steps, I heard a sweet voice greet me – a voice that echoed the smile that graced the face of the speaker. I turned and saw a beautiful, yet road-worn woman, something younger than myself, sitting on Barb O's porch swing.

I returned her greeting and flashed an equally genuine smile as I continued into the diner. Had I not been so achingly hungry, I would have stopped and chatted a bit with the woman but my stomach was my master and my master drove me on through the doors. Barb O's is a typical diner-style restaurant with a long coffee bar lined with red vinyl covered stools. A dozen or so tables were placed about the dining room all surrounded by chairs with the same blood red covering on the seat cushions. As I had feared, business was slack that day and only a scattering of people idled in the dining area.

I was immediately the center of attention. My hair was much longer then that it is now and certainly longer than anyone in the room. I had an old guitar and an even older rucksack slung over my back and several miles of wet road pasted to my clothes. As is often the case in back road diners, the patrons of Barb O's soon lost interest in me but I knew that I was constantly within their peripheral vision as I approached the counter and asked the waitress at the cash register if I could speak to the manager.

"Manager," laughed the heavy woman, identified as Dorlene by the embroidery on her uniform. "You got a complaint or somethin', honey?"

"No," I replied. "I have a business proposition.

Dorlene looked hard at me, presumably reading my face for sincerity, while she snapped a large wad of gum.

"Well, the manager is Harlan, my husband. He ain't here. Why don't you tell me your story and I'll see if he might be interested?"

I explained to Dorlene who I was and what I was looking to do. I described my past three days in colorful detail and told her that I would be more than happy to wash dishes, sweep floors, clean out dumpsters or even sit and sing a few songs, in exchange for a hot meal or two. Dorlene listened to my story and when I finished pleading my case she stopped snapping her gum and raised her eyes toward the front door.

"She with you?" She asked, nodding toward the door.

I turned around to see that the young lady from the porch swing had quietly entered the diner and was standing in a beam of brilliant sunlight with her arms held demurely behind her back. I looked into those eyes. My God what eyes! I saw the miles of road that clung to her as it did to me. I felt my heart slip and for a brief moment, my hunger abated. I stammered for an answer and somehow managed to respond, albeit feebly.

"She's, um," I said, turning back to Dorlene. "She's…"

"I don't want to know," Dorlene interrupted, putting up her hand to stop me. "You two are pretty young so if she's your girlfriend or your wife or your sister, it's all the same to me. She pregnant?"

That slapped me hard, I'll tell you! I didn't know this girl. I was not sure what was really happening at that point. I had never before felt so disoriented in my life. I must have been quite a sight with my jaw hanging open! Behind me, the girl giggled a bit and then answered the question that had so tongue-tied me.

"No, but we're trying."

I turned to face the girl who threw me a sly but comforting wink.

"Tory and I aren't married yet," she continued. "But we plan on getting to Vegas and getting married in the Elvis Chapel!"

I felt my face flush at the mention of my middle name. I couldn't figure out how she knew me and how she was able to so quickly fabricate such an obscure story. After a moment I realized that she must have heard me introduce myself to Dorlene and used my middle name to create a sense of familiarity for the woman. Later, I learned that she was the daughter of a writer and knew that the fallacious story was the product of a genetically creative mind. You should be proud, sir!

I caught my breath, felt the flush drain from my face, and turned back to Dorlene.

"We've been on the road for a while. Traveling to…"

"California," the girl interrupted.

"California," I repeated.

Dorlene gave me that hard testing glare and then switched her focus to the girl behind me. I think it was the sight of the girl that softened Dorlene's resolve, as I was pretty sure she was going to give me the boot before she came through the door.

"Shoot," she said after a few moments of deep thought. "Business is in the shitter and I go and take on a sob case like this. All right you two, come with me."

Dorlene turned and marched through the swinging doors into the kitchen. The young girl followed quickly but as she passed by me she leaned close and whispered a single, beautiful word.

"Jenna."

I watched her walk into the kitchen and disappear behind the doors. I stood motionless for a moment, feeling overpowered, swept up in the currents of destiny. I must have made quite an amusing sight as I soon became aware that the meager patrons of Barb O's were laughing and offering encouragement for me to follow. I replied with a flustered smile and pushed on through the kitchen doors.

Dorlene was tying an apron around Jenna when I found them in the back. Jenna looked up when I entered and gave me another wink. I smiled in return and then scanned the back room to see what kind of work might need to be done.

"You know much about cars?" Dorlene asked, fidgeting with a knot that had fixed itself in the apron string.

"Fair amount," I replied.

"Engines?"

"Some, I guess. Older cars more than the new fuel-injected models."

"Good," Dorlene returned with a smile, finally conquering the knot.

"There's a buggy out back with your name on it. Get that kitten to purr and I'll put enough meat and potatoes in you to get you to Vegas. Your lady friend and I will be servin' up whoever comes in the door. What did you say your name was again?"

"His name's Tory," Jenna replied and I felt my heart slip again as her beautiful mouth formed my name.

It's strange. I had always gone by Angus until that day. It's an obscure enough name to make it memorable. Still, I endured as much ridicule as fascination with that name, particularly in cow country. With such a simple gesture she changed forever the way people would think of me, and the way I would think of myself.

"Well, Tory," Dorlene continued. "Get out there and

see what you can do. Take one of those sandwiches in the fridge to quiet that stomach of yours. For God's sakes boy you're growling like a rusty muffler."

She tossed me a ring of keys and pointed to the back door.

Several cars littered the back yard of Barb O's. The buggy, a black 1967 Impala, was the only one that wasn't either up on blocks or so firmly embedded in the ground as to become more of a box garden for weeds than anything else. The Impala was the only vehicle that still had four tires.

I hoped that the problem was with starting, as I had neither the tools nor the expertise to fix a transmission if the latter were the issue. I plopped down on the big bench front seat and slid the ignition key in. Tentatively turning it forward, I listened for any telltale sounds that might identify the problem. The engine responded with a spinning whine. The battery was all right, as was the starter. The problem was either fuel or air. I could fix that, but I needed some tools. As if she had heard my thought, Dorlene appeared clutching a large, heavy-looking tool chest in her meaty hand.

"You might find it easier with these," she said.

I thanked her and told her what I suspected the problem was.

"Don't make no difference to me. If you can fix it, you're my hero. If not...well...I'll probably feed you anyway. That lady of yours sure can make me laugh."

Dorlene returned to the restaurant and I returned to my work. After a few hours of stripping down and cleaning the carburetor, and checking the fuel lines, I was startled by a loud cough behind me. I turned and saw an enormous man, who could only be Harlan, standing by the door smoking an equally large cigar. His girth easily matched his height and he was not short. His hair was pulled back in a sweep of greasy, thinning strands, revealing an overabundance of forehead, and he was dressed in cook's whites from head to toe. Everything about the man was big which made him appear more of a professional wrestler than a chef.

"You Tory?" The man coughed.

"Yes. You Harlan?" I replied.

The man spit a piece of tobacco toward his feet and then returned the big stogy to his mouth.

"Yeah. 'Spose I am."

I wiped my greasy, gasoline scented hands off on a piece of rag I'd found in the toolbox and offered it to the mountain of a man. Harlan returned the gesture, using the sleeve of his shirt to dry off his palm. My hand vanished in his grip.

"You think you can fix that piece o' shit?" Harlan asked through his cigar.

I assured him that I could once I had cleaned the carburetor and replaced the fuel line. I also informed him that I didn't carry a spare fuel line for a '67 Impala in my rucksack. He looked at me suspiciously.

"You're not Gordy's new kid?" He asked.

Despite the look in his eye and his superior mass I had to deny even knowing anyone named Gordy. I wondered if maybe Dorlene had told him some story so that he'd accept a stranger working on his car.

"Damn woman. Your name *is* Tory, right?"

"Yes."

"Dorlene!" Harlan bellowed, turning his head toward the back door but keeping his eyes planted on me. Dorlene appeared a few seconds later.

"Who is this kid?" Harlan asked, pointing the business end of his cigar at me.

"I told you," Dorlene snapped.

"Yeah, you told me his name and you also told me he was Gordy's new mechanic."

Dorlene remained silent, as did I. Finally, I think she realized that Harlan's statement was really a question. Dorlene admitted who I was and why she had me fixing the Chevy. Her own story consisted of a bit of my own, most of Jenna's, and some embellishment of her own that I think she hoped would soften the big man to our need.

To his credit, Harlan listened to the entire story, puffing on his cigar as he sized me up. When she finished, he stood quiet for a minute, apparently letting the story sink in, but kept his eyes locked on me.

"You sure you can fix this shitbox?" Harlan said, finally breaking the unnerving silence.

"Yes," I replied a little over-enthusiastically. "But, I'll need a fuel line."

"Fuel line." Harlan repeated, spitting another piece of tobacco toward the ground.

Dorlene seemed a little uneasy which was contagious when standing so close to such a large man. I waited for Harlan to make some sort of decision regarding my continued efforts. He tossed the cigar back and forth between the puffy corners of his mouth as he thought over the situation.

"Jesus H. The things I do for you woman," he said at last.

"You better get in the truck boy and hope to Hell Gordy's got a fuel line up to his place."

We drove in silence for several miles on a back road to a place that was a veritable museum of junk cars. Gordy – the owner – had plenty of spare parts including the necessary parts for the Impala.

Harlan told Gordy I was fixing up "Dorlene's shitbox Chevy" which brought a scowl to the face of the man. I guess Gordy must have wanted the job or perhaps felt threatened that someone else was performing auto repair work on his turf. Either way I didn't feel welcome, but I did feel somewhat safe standing next to Harlan – an ironic twist considering how intimidated I had been only a half hour earlier.

On the ride back, Harlan asked about me and my travels and I told him roughly the same story that I related to you two in the beginning of this letter. He asked me about Jenna. I dodged the direct question and instead provided a generic piece of double-talk and turned the conversation back onto Dorlene and himself. I think he caught my evasion but he made no attempt to pursue the question. He talked about his wife and their relationship, particularly how it had been in the beginning and how they were still friends if not lovers after all these years. He talked about the restaurant, how his mother Barb Oster started it and how he had taken up the reigns after she died.

He enjoyed talking. I enjoyed listening.

It was nearly dinnertime when we returned to Barb O's but the sun still had miles to go across the sky so I returned to the Impala despite the grumbling of my stomach. Sitting on top of the car were two sandwiches and two Cokes. The cans were ice cold and sweating in the humid air. A note was under one of the cans that read, simply:

Thought you might like a snack before you get your fill of meat and potatoes!
Jenna

I was extremely touched by the gesture and Harlan laughed, saying that Dorlene was always thinking with his stomach, as he grabbed one of the sandwiches and all but shoved it into his wide mouth. I let him think that Dorlene was the one that left the snacks. I could tell he truly loved her despite his grumbling.

With the sandwiches gone and the Coke being nursed for every drop of cold refreshment, I completed the work on the car under the casual supervision of Harlan, who sat it an over-stressed lawn chair.

When I finally sat in the driver's seat and turned over the key I was famished and exhausted but relieved that I had been able to get the car together before sunset. The engine spun a bit, wheezed a bit, but then caught and coughed out a cloud of black, oily smoke. Harlan got up out of his seat much to the relief of the chair I'm sure. His face was plastered with a wide smile and he expressed his satisfaction with two words repeated over and over.

"Hot shit!"

I told him that although the car was running, it was still not safe to drive very far and he would want Gordy to perform a full tune-up on it as soon as possible.

Dorlene, needless to say, was as happy as a clam to hear the engine roar to life. She and Harlan climbed into the car, much to the displeasure of the groaning shock absorbers. I watched them for a few minutes, seeing the old newness of their relationship climb back to the surface if only for a few minutes. Behind me I heard whispered praise for the major effect of a minor effort.

"Well done, hubby. I hope you're hungry?"

I turned to respond but she was gone from the door. What a strange creature, this Jenna!

Dorlene told me to go into the restaurant and get cleaned up. I was more than happy to oblige as I am not fond of the texture of motor oil, and besides I wanted to secure a few minutes alone with Jenna so we could at least get our stories synchronized. I had no idea what she had been telling Dorlene about me so I wanted to be sure not to make either of us look like fools, particularly if we were going to be well fed. And of course talking with her face to face would give me another chance to look into those eyes!

I found soap and a towel in the small washroom off the storage room and set to removing God knows how many years of oil and grime I had bathed in while working on the car. As I scrubbed I listened for an indication of how busy the diner was. It was well into the dinner rush but the only sound coming from the dining area was an occasional clink of silverware on a plate. Dorlene had mentioned in her own colorful way that business had not been good. I felt somewhat guilty asking for what I considered a free meal from these people.

Back in the kitchen I ran into Jenna busily scraping the charred remains of a hamburger off the griddle. It was strange. I knew nothing about her but I seemed to know everything I needed. I watched as she scraped, pausing between strokes to brush the hair from her eyes. A smudge of blackened grease had found its way to her forehead creating a third eyebrow. I grabbed a hand towel and walked over to where she worked. She looked up at me as I approached. Without speaking, I used the towel to wipe the grease from her face. I was dumbstruck. I wanted to talk to her, ask her about herself, but I couldn't find the words. She looked at the towel as I pulled it away and then lifted her face to me.

I'm sure as her parents you know full well the brightness of Jenna's smiling face. She doesn't smile with only her mouth. Instead, her entire face lights up and her eyes emit a kind of sparkle that can only come from a truly happy soul. That is the face that looked up at me that day. That is the face that remains engraved in my memory.

Jenna didn't speak in those few consuming moments either. She simply smiled at me then returned to her scraping. I stood back, wondering for a moment if I should break the silence and try to find out just who she and I were supposed to be to these people. I found a drinking glass and poured myself some water, trying to find the words I needed to open up a conversation with her. Jenna found them before me.

"I told Dorlene the truth," she said without looking up. "I told her that you and I don't really know each other; that it was just a little play I put on to get a meal as well. I've been on the road for quite a while and I ran out of money and food a couple of days ago. I hope you don't mind."

"I don't mind," I said. "I enjoyed the ruse."

Jenna stopped her scraping and looked up grinning. It wasn't the same smile that I had seen before but it was equally as beautiful.

"Nobody uses that word; *ruse*. Daddy would like you."

"Daddy?"

"Daddy. Father. Male parental unit. You know the term?"

Jenna's sarcasm is, I'm sorry, was incisive. She said she got that from you ma'am.

I assured her that I knew the term but was merely prompting her to continue about her father. I have never been very good at asking personal questions. I feel that most things are none of my business and if people want to talk about them, they'll do so without my asking. Being with Jenna has taught me to be more open.

She told me about you, sir – that you're a writer and that you live in Mertztown, PA. That was when I first mentioned the Fred and Ethel gag. It was quite an icebreaker and in the moments when we were both laughing, I knew a friendship had been forged.

But before our conversation could continue any further, Dorlene and Harlan came into the kitchen both with smiles pasted to their wide faces and faraway looks in their eyes. Harlan even had a smudge of lipstick by his ear. I tossed him the towel that I had used to wipe the grease from Jenna's face and then pointed to my own ear to indicate the location of the smudge.

"Well, sir," Dorlene said, straightening out the wrinkles in her uniform. "I do think that this has been an interesting day. Wouldn't you agree Harlan?"

"A very interesting day," Harlan agreed, throwing a knowing wink to his wife.

"You know, Tory, that old buggy was the car that Harlan drove to pick me up on our very first date. It hasn't run in quite a while and I was beginning to think that our marriage was as stalled as its old engine. Seems old Harlan here needed nothing more than a good cleaning and a new fuel line."

Harlan blushed at his wife's analogy.

"Now hush up, Dorlene. These kids don't want to hear about my uncontrollable animal magnetism. They're hungry."

Dorlene agreed and sent the two of us to the dining room to wait for our meal. I was grateful for the break and for the opportunity to talk more with Jenna. But, Jenna beat me to the punch and began speaking before we had even said down.

"Do you always make people so happy?" She asked.

"I guess I try," I told her. "I had no idea that fixing up that old Chevy would stir up such feelings in those two. I kind of got this feeling that Harlan was something of a hard case."

Jenna nodded and then prompted me for my story. I

began with the death of my parents and my subsequent journey from Columbia, SC, in search of my destiny. I told her about the long stretches of road and the truckers – both kinds. I told her about my trips to the libraries and my thirst for experience.

Jenna sat quietly, leaning her head against her hand, her beautiful blonde hair flowing down over the wrist to rest lightly on the tabletop. I had been talking for a straight half hour when Dorlene brought out our meals.

When I saw the amount of food they had prepared, I felt my jaw drop. Roast beef, mashed potatoes and gravy, green beans, corn on the cob, carrots, a loaf of homemade bread with real butter to plaster on it, side salads with big scoops of cottage cheese and ice cold beer to wash it all down.

Jenna and I tore into the feast, hardly speaking a word until our momentum slowed a bit. We clinked our beer glasses together in celebration of our new friendship with each other and the renewed love affair of Harlan and Dorlene. Our benefactors joined us for dessert – thick slices of Dorlene's trademark chocolate layer cake buried under a mound of vanilla ice cream. The thick black coffee I spoke of earlier did little to help wash down the clods of cake and ice cream, but it went well with the dessert and despite the overabundance of caffeine, we each downed several cups.

When dinner and dessert were over, Harlan locked up the front door and walked over to an old jukebox in the corner. I had not even noticed it until Harlan pushed it away from the wall and slid his big paw down behind it. With a flick of a switch the box jumped into life with a flash of multi-colored lights bulbs. The big man selected several songs, mostly slow ones, and then returned to his wife who had cleared away the dessert plates while he fumbled with the machine. Harlan put his thick arm around his wife's waist and began to rock back and forth. In no time the two were dancing as close as their abundant bellies would allow, but close enough to find something in each other's eyes.

I watched Jenna watching them. I saw a tear form and flow slowly down her cheek and knew that the sentiment of the moment was not lost on her. As I watched, her smile faded and became an almost imperceptible frown.

"What's wrong?" I asked her.

She replied with a shake of her head and then turned around to sit properly in the booth, facing away from the two dancers. I was confused. A moment like that is something special. I tried to get her to open up in order to see what it was that had so saddened her. Her reply only furthered my confusion.

"I have never known that kind of emotion," she said. "I probably never will."

As I said before, I've never been very good at getting personal with people. I didn't know how to pursue the conversation in order to get her to voice her sorrow so I sat in silence, watching her.

On the jukebox, the music continued. On the dining room floor, the dance continued. When the song changed and James Taylor began crooning through his rendition of *Up On the Roof*, I asked Jenna if she would like to join Harlan and Dorlene on the dance floor. I'm not much of a dancer and being so forward as to ask a woman to dance is out of my nature, but I felt at that moment in time it was the right thing and before I knew it the words were out of my mouth and into her ears.

Jenna stared at me for a few moments sizing up the sincerity of my invitation, I imagine. Without a word she agreed by reaching her hand across the table. I took it in my own, thrilling to the energy of that first touch, and led her out between the tables with their scarlet covered chairs.

That first dance was a chaste effort. An icebreaker. We held each other modestly looking into the other's face. About halfway through the last chorus a smile carved its way across Jenna's face. Her eyes, which had been filled with sadness, brightened.

"You're some kind of catalyst," she said.

I withheld a response, as well as a crack about being put in the same classification as an enzyme. I don't respond to compliments very well. At least I didn't at that point. Since then, Jenna taught me to simply say "thank you" and shut up.

On the juke, JT's milky voice faded and the song changed. John Fogerty began belting out the piteous strains of the workingman's blues. The tempo changed. The dance changed. And the entire atmosphere of Barb O's seemed to brighten. During the chorus, the air was filled with the voice of the four of us pleading the *Midnight Special* to shine its ever-lovin' light on us.

Harlan went to the kitchen for more beers and Dorlene went to the juke to program some more music and the dancing and drinking continued.

By midnight, we had all had our share of alcohol and moldy oldies. Harlan told us that we could sleep in the back room of the kitchen if we wanted to, and then he and Dorlene took their leave of us giggling like a couple of flirtatious teenagers as they locked the door behind them.

Jenna led the way to the back room which was really nothing more than an empty pantry. There was enough room for both of us to curl up on the floor but I chose to sleep outside the little room. Although I wanted to be close to her, I did not want to seem opportunistic. So I pulled my tattered blanket from my pack and lay down by the doorway, hoping to have a little sleep over chatter with Jenna before finally falling prey to the Sandman. My wish went unfulfilled, as Jenna, exhausted from the beer and the dancing, was asleep within minutes of stretching out.

I stared at the darkened ceiling of the kitchen. Dorlene had been right. It certainly had been an interesting day. My mind wandered as I rehashed the events of the day and eventually sleep consumed me.

March 14 – Dayton, OH

As you can see from the date, I've been on the move again. I managed to catch a ride to Toledo and then hitched down to Dayton. I don't have any real reason to be here but that's the way it is on the road. You get to where you're going even if you don't know where that is!

I read what I've written so far so I could get back in the rhythm of the story. Again I had an urge to rework some of the pages but it's truthful and accurate to my memory so again, I'll let it sit.

I woke the next morning as the sun cleared the horizon. Sleeping outdoors as often as I do, has made me sensitive to the arrival of morning. Jenna was still sleeping off the beer on the pantry floor. I watched her for a few minutes listening to the rhythm of her breathing and again felt something slip within me.

I suppose I should try to explain that "slipping" feeling. It is like joy and despair in the same breath – like falling in love and losing your best friend all in one. I knew there was something special about Jenna but there was also something tragic. But after only one day of her company I was incapable of identifying either.

I rolled up my blanket and returned it to my rucksack.

While the sack was open I retrieved my sketchpad and pencils. Barb O's would not open for a couple of hours. I figured Harlan and/or Dorlene would be in at least an hour early to get the coffee thickening and the grease sizzling. I had to hurry if I wanted to finish the sketch before they arrived.

The back door opened onto a glorious day. The layer of clouds had burned away and the sun sat on the horizon lighting everything with that ethereal golden-pink morning light. I walked around the Impala until I found the perfect angle where the light was just right and the shadows perfect. I plopped myself on the ground and began drawing.

The fresh morning air and bluing sky awakened the artist within me and I felt myself slip into the trance-like state where the Maestro within me can work. The Impala flowed out of the page, materializing with each stroke of graphite. I worked at the drawing finding the light and shadow, sharpening the ends of my shortened pencils, pulling each detail from the surface of the blank page. In the end I had captured an excellent representation of Harlan's old love machine, if I do say so myself. Through the glare of the windshield the hazy shape of Harlan, somewhat thinner than his current bulk, leaned over to kiss an equally blurred Dorlene. Satisfied with the work, I signed the drawing with my characteristic scrawl along the lower right edge of the drawing then returned to the kitchen.

Jenna sat on the counter spooning milk sodden scoops of cereal into her mouth. She greeted me with a wan smile as I entered the kitchen and then tapped her middle finger to her forehead indicating the dull throb of a hangover. She obviously didn't handle the beer as well as she had hoped. As I walked by her, intending to place the drawing on the desk in Harlan's office, she caught a glimpse of the sketch and demanded through a dripping mouthful of cereal to see it.

I have had people tell me that they liked my work before but words alone fall flat compared to the look on Jenna's face as she examined the drawing. I watched her. The emotions that crossed her face and the almost imperceptible shake of her head revealed more to me about how the drawing affected her than if she had simply told me, "I like it." After a few minutes of scrutiny, she handed the paper back to me and voiced her approval.

"You're a catalyst."

I took this as a compliment and was about to voice my appreciation when Harlan walked in grinning from ear to ear and threw me a sly wink.

"Boy, if I had known how much Dorlene missed that old Chevy, I would have had it fixed years ago."

Jenna burst out laughing and congratulated Harlan on his renewed romance.

"If she liked that, she'll love this."

She pointed to the drawing that I held slightly behind my back, and away from Harlan. Harlan craned his thick neck as well as anyone of his dimension can to see what it was I held behind me.

The jig was up. The surprise was lost. I handed the sketch over.

Harlan stared at the sketch for several minutes before

quietly walking into his office. As he walked his eyes never left the drawing. I watched him disappear into the office and heard the groan of his chair as he sat down at the desk.

Jenna put her hand on my shoulder and pulled me around.

"What are your plans for today?"

I told her that I planned on hitting the road after I had worked off a breakfast. She told me that she thought I had already done that and offered to make me something. I accepted.

Jenna had a way of automatically knowing her boundaries in any situation. She knew that it would be all right with Harlan if we made ourselves something to eat without asking. I have never been so confident in determining my level of acceptance with others. The ease with which she moved through her life and relationships was impressive.

I stood next to the griddle as Jenna fried some eggs and sausage for me. We talked about the previous night, the drawing, and Harlan and Dorlene. I asked her what *her* plans were for the day, assuming that they were different from my own. She told me that she wasn't sure. She mentioned the need to contact you two but she was hesitant to use the telephone for fear that hearing your voices would bring on too many emotions she didn't want to deal with yet. She thought she might stick around another day and help Dorlene with the restaurant provided Dorlene thought she needed help. Our conversation was interrupted by Harlan who stood in the doorway of his office holding the drawing in his large hands.

"You two are welcome to stick around and work today," he said. "Business ain't great so I can't pay you, but I'm happy to feed you."

We both agreed to stick around which brought a smile to his wide face.

We spent that day helping out around the restaurant. Jenna waited tables and took her turn at the griddle. I kept the floors and rest rooms clean, which wasn't hard as there were only a dozen or so customers all day. Harlan took the drawing into town and came back a few hours later with the picture matted and framed. He hung it on his office wall and periodically during the day he and Dorlene would sneak into the office to look at it and reminisce. Although they never actually said anything about the picture, other than "thank you," their actions spoke for them and I was gratified that I had given them something so meaningful.

Just after lunch I snuck out back with a bucket of water, some soap, and a can of Turtle Wax I'd found on a shelf in the main pantry. I spent an hour cleaning and waxing the Impala, bringing back as much of the old beast as I could. I think there is a certain Zen to these types of chores as the mindless motion of the arms allows the brain to focus on more esoteric things.

It dawned on me as I buffed the hood and front quarter panels that the car was a kind of physical representation of Harlan and Dorlene's love for each other – a totem of sorts. When the old Chevy had stalled, so had the intensity of their romance. Bringing the car back to life put the charge back into their relationship. I wondered if other relationships had similar physical icons and decided that I would try to look for those in the future.

As evening drew near, I felt it was time I moved on. Dorlene insisted that I stay another night but I told her that despite the attractiveness of the offer I felt the need to keep moving. Harlan understood my need but also voiced his desire for me to stay. I thanked them both for their kindness and told them that I would likely see them again some day, especially after having another slice of that chocolate cake! Harlan assured me that as long as Barb O's was in business I was welcome to throw down a sandwich and a beer anytime.

I packed up my rucksack, slung it and Erik over my shoulder, and said my final good-byes to the two. Dorlene hugged my tightly and once again I saw my hand disappear into Harlan's great paw. Jenna was not in the kitchen or the dining area but I found her on the porch swing just where I had first seen her on the previous day.

"Leaving?" She asked.

"Yeah," I said. "Time to move on. I want to try to get across the desert before it gets too hot this summer. Can't stay long in any one place."

Jenna nodded and then stood and approached me.

"Thank you," she said. "For me, for them. You're an interesting person Tory McLeod. I'm happy I got to meet you."

Then she hugged me and walked into the restaurant. I had hoped that she would like to leave with me but felt uncomfortable about making the offer.

I made my way to the road and in the dwindling light of the dying day I stuck my thumb out and proceeded to inch my way north. I was several miles outside Salina, the crossroads where I would begin heading west, before I decided to rest for the night. I'd had no luck at all in securing a ride with the few cars and trucks that passed by that evening. Still the walk was nice. The moon had come up and lit the surrounding landscape with its ghostly glow. The weather had stayed fair and the sky was littered with a few puffy clouds but for the most part the stars shone down on me as I walked on.

I had just decided to veer off the road into a cluster of trees for the night when I heard the roar of an engine behind me and turned to see the headlights of a pickup truck barreling down the road behind me.

One last try, I thought and stuck out my thumb. The pickup rolled down the long straight road toward me, then passed me without even slowing down. I was half glad that the truck had not stopped as I spied two young men, probably locals and definitely drunk, shouting at each other and the night from the bed of the truck. I could only guess that the cab contained an equal number of rowdies, most likely just as drunk as the two in the back.

I watched the truck plunge into the darkness, a single working taillight becoming a red dot racing along the highway. I was about to proceed with my plan to camp for the night when I noticed the truck slow down and then stop about a quarter-mile down the road. The passenger door opened, slammed shut and the truck sped off toward the horizon.

When the truck stopped, I was certain that I was in for a night of cat and mouse with the drunken passengers. As I stated earlier, I have had my share of run-ins with that type in the past. I was at an advantage in this situation as it was dark and I had time to bolt for cover it they decided to come back for me.

But when the truck rolled on, that single taillight becoming smaller and smaller, I breathed easier but wondered why it had stopped in the first place. My confusion was soon set straight as I saw a shape coming out of the darkness walking toward me. As the person drew closer I recognized the shape and then the face as the moon shone down on that perfect smile and that flowing blonde hair. It was Jenna!

As she approached, she reached into the pocket of her oversized denim jacket and withdrew a can of beer.

"Fancy meeting you here, McLeod!" She shouted, handing the can over to me.

I was awed and delighted that she was standing once again before me. I commented on how funny fate can be as it was surely fate that put us on the same road to cross paths once again. Had the truck driven by a minute later, I would have been safely in the scrub setting out my blanket for the night.

Instead of camping alone I had a friend to share the night. We moved off the road into the trees and set up a small campfire. As I laid out my blanket and Jenna her own bedroll she told me that she had spotted me as the truck rolled past and demanded that the driver, someone called "Arco" by the boys in the back, let her out. She said that the three had picked her up at Barb O's and offered to take her to Salina. As soon as she was in the truck, Arco offered her one of the many beers on the seat of the cab. She declined but managed to sneak a few in her coat without him noticing. She wanted to remain clear headed while she was in the company of three teenagers whose judgment and inhibitions were impaired.

I told her of my unsuccessful attempt to land a ride since leaving Barb O's. I also confessed that I had not really made the most complete effort, as I was thinking about her and wondering what it would have been like to travel with her.

"I guess you'll find out now!" She replied with that beautiful smile. "Good thing you didn't hitch a ride or I might never have caught up with you."

I stared at her for a minute, watching the firelight dance over her face. She had come after me! My heart soared but I kept my joy silent, as I was still unsure of her motivation. I could only hope...

We talked for an hour or so, sharing tales of the road. We decided that it would be better if we traveled together, at least until she got to her goal. I had no particular objective in mind, save for wandering the forests of Central California, so it was easy to agree on a destination.

Silence fell over us as we settled back on our respective bedrolls. I watched the flickering firelight and felt my heart beating against my chest. For the first time in my life I actually felt alive! I was not merely a wandering entity. I was a living man. I felt the earth beneath me, and the warmth of the fire on my face. I saw the stars shining through the broken canopy of the trees. I felt and heard the warm June breeze swirl around me and breathed in the scents it carried. But mostly I felt something inside – something welling up from somewhere so deep within me that it seemed to come from miles and miles away. Something about this woman had set that all in motion.

"Tory," Jenna said softly.

I turned toward her and acknowledged her call.

"Don't...don't fall in love with me. Promise?"

My heart stopped. It was as if she had read my mind and then denied me the thoughts and feelings that came so naturally. I was crushed. I could not answer and felt it best that I couldn't. I could not lie to her and accept the request and the oath, but at the same time I could not decline it. She needed to keep me distant and I couldn't accept that either. But that night was not the night to discuss it so I simply rolled over and willed myself to sleep.

Interlude
Dorlene

June 16, 1994
Dear Mr. McCormick,

    Now I know what it's like to be drowning at sea. One wave crashes over you and just as you think you're about to catch your breath, another wave comes along. Your letter felt like that to me. I don't blame you. You couldn't possibly know.
    It's just that Harlan passed away this spring. His big old heart just couldn't keep up with his big old body. He had his first heart attack in February and we thought that was going to be the end, but when he made it through and was released from the hospital, we thought we had surely dodged a bullet. The final attack in March took him in his sleep so at least I have that to be thankful for.
    I was just coming to grips with his passing when I received your letter. I'm so sorry to hear about Jenna. I had no idea she was ill when she was here. She was such a funny sweet girl. We had a fine time when she and Tory were here even if it was just for a couple of days. They both had such a great influence on Harlan and me. I half expected we would be seeing them again some day. I guess that won't be the case at least as far as Jenna goes.
    I haven't seen Tory since then. I hope to some day. Now that I have your information, I'll be sure to get in touch if I ever do. I'll also be sure to tell him that you're

looking for him. Please be sure to let me know if you find him first. I should like to give him Harlan's old Impala if he would take it. Fixing that old buggy made Harlan happier than anything I can remember. I know he would want Tory to have it. Harlan talked about that boy every day as if he was his own.

You have my deepest sympathy for the loss of your daughter.

    Take care and God bless you,
    Dorlene Oster

    P.S. I've enclosed a picture of the drawing Tory did for us. That boy has a gift.

Continuation
Back on the Road

March 15 – Troy, OH

I woke suddenly feeling a weight on my lungs. I opened my eyes to see the grinning idiot face of a teenage boy looking down at me as he knelt on my chest.

"This one's awake Arco."

Arco! That was the name of the driver of the truck that had picked Jenna up. They had come back and must have spotted our campfire. I looked toward the road and saw the pickup truck parked haphazardly on the shoulder.

"Keep him still, P. Roy," came a deeper voice, most likely Arco's from the other side of the campfire – the side where Jenna was asleep.

I tried to call out, to warn Jenna, but a dirty hand clamped over my mouth from behind. A third hoodlum was kneeling near my head, helping P. Roy keep me incapacitated.

As he knelt on me, looking back and forth between Arco and me, P. Roy took large gulps from a beer can, the same brand as the one Jenna had handed me. I tried to move my arms, to throw him off me but found that my arms were crossed beneath me, pinned by my own weight and that of the kneeler. The boy who held my mouth began to play games with me, pinching my nose for long periods of time, only to let go and laugh while I struggled to breathe.

On the other side of the fire I heard a whisper, then a shout and a struggle. This Arco character was doing something to Jenna, but I couldn't see what.

P. Roy and his idiot companion watched Arco in dazed fascination as the brute continued his assault on Jenna. I heard Jenna's curses and knew that she was fighting with all she had, but I was afraid this Arco character, who I had not yet seen, would overpower her and exact whatever toll *he* felt was fair for the ride he had given her. Jenna screamed out my name and I replied with a bellow of anguish muffled by the grubby fingers of the creep behind me.

P. Roy looked down at me when Jenna called out. His empty eyes, glazed over with drunken depravity, glared at me.

"Tory?" He said, pouring part of his beer over my face. "That your name, boy?"

"What kinda faggot name is that?" Number Three said behind me.

Jenna screamed again and I heard cloth tearing.

"Get 'er, Arco!" P. Roy cheered.

From beyond P. Roy's eclipsing form I heard Arco swear and then heard the slap of an open hand. I hoped that the slapping hand was Jenna's and not Arco's. More cloth tearing then Jenna shouted one last time.

"I have AIDS!"

The clearing fell silent. P. Roy loomed above me slack jawed staring in the direction of his friend. The third goon behind me loosened his grip on my mouth. I was even dumbstruck. I knew that Jenna was capable of spontaneous fabrication but this declaration of hers really took the cake!

"Bullshit," I heard Arco say.

"Try me," Jenna replied in icy defiance.

"That true?" Arco shouted in my direction.

"That true?" P. Roy repeated, looking to me as if I would tell the truth if I knew it.

"Yes," I replied quietly, playing along with Jenna's ploy. P. Roy looked back at his friend and repeated what I had said.

Number Three seemed to pull away from me as if I was infected with the same dread disease that Jenna claimed. Arco must have backed away from Jenna, as she was soon standing near enough for me to see her face.

"Get off him!" She shouted.

P. Roy turned his head away from Jenna as if he could contract the disease simply by looking at her.

"I said get off him. Get off him now, or so help me I'll bite you!"

P. Roy stood up relieving the pressure from my chest and arms. I managed to pull my numb, aching limbs out from under me and rise to my knees. It was then that I caught my first glimpse of Arco. He was no older that seventeen or eighteen but he was big. Probably played football for his high school. Jenna wouldn't have been a match for him if she hadn't scared him off with her grim announcement.

I rose to my feet still unable to move my aching arms. I felt hate course through me. I am usually a very peaceful, non-violent soul, but at that moment I wanted nothing more than to bury my foot in Arco's face. Jenna stood beside me and calmed me with a touch of her hand on my throbbing arm.

P. Roy must have seen the look in my eyes as he quickly backed off. Number Three followed suit. Arco stood by sizing us both up. I don't think he believed Jenna's story and the alcohol in his system was still in control of his better judgment.

"This is bullshit," Arco said finally. "P. Roy, Trip, hold his ass again. I'm gonna finish what I started with this pretty bitch."

P. Roy dropped his beer and made a move to follow Arco's orders. Number Three, smaller than his friend and now identified as Trip, fell in behind P. Roy while Arco stepped toward Jenna.

Jenna poised herself for battle and I mentally cocked my foot in preparation for P. Roy's attack. I doubted that I'd be able to take Arco in a one-on-one fight, but with Jenna and me both at him, combined with the alcohol in his system, I was certain we could make stand. But before I could do that, I had to take care of P. Roy and Trip.

I was just about to initiate the action when the flashing blue and red lights of a police cruiser erased the necessity of battle. All three of our assailants looked toward the flashing lights then back at each other. All of them, including Arco, were suddenly nervous by this new addition to our camp. I watched as a tall, thin man silhouetted by the rolling lights stepped out of the cruiser and walked toward the pick-up truck.

"Break out some ID kiddies," the man said as he searched the open bed and cab of the truck with a bright flashlight. "The Law's here."

The man's voice was heavy with a Southern drawl, not the characteristic flat twang of Middle America. He was not from Kansas. Not originally anyway. I was willing to bet he was from the Carolina's like me.

Arco, P. Roy, and Trip all reached for their wallets. Jenna retrieved her ID from her backpack. I had no ID whatsoever and suddenly felt a bit of jail time coming on.

The tall man walked away from the pick-up truck and entered the clearing. As he approached P. Roy he bent down and picked up the half empty can of beer at the boy's feet.

"This yours, son?" He asked P. Roy.

P. Roy shook his head and pointed toward me. The officer turned in my direction and gave me a once over in the flickering firelight. He then turned back to P. Roy and pressed the question.

"You sure this ain't yours? I could have it checked for fingerprints you know? Wouldn't go very good for you if you're lyin' to an officer of the law, now would it?"

P. Roy remained silent. The officer must have realized that he was not going to get anywhere with P. Roy so he looked at Trip instead. As he questioned the smaller boy I noticed Arco stepping back into the shadows. The officer must have heard him moving as he turned quickly around and pinned him with a stare.

"I think I'd like you to sit down right where you're standing," he said pointing at the ground below Arco's feet.

Arco stood defiantly for a few moments and then sat down on the ground. The officer turned back to P. Roy and Trip and collected their IDs. He instructed them to also sit on the ground. He then collected Arco's ID and made a quick comment on the boy's size and how he must play football. Then he turned to Jenna and me.

Jenna easily handed over her identification but I had nothing to give. I told the officer that I had lost my wallet quite a while ago, which was true. He looked hard at me and I couldn't tell if he believed me or not. After a minute or so he turned and walked toward the campfire shining his flashlight on the identification cards. I was surprised that he didn't ask Jenna or me to sit down as well.

"Carl Martin Burger," the officer said loudly. Trip responded with a weak "yes sir."

"Purcevil Roy Granger."

P. Roy responded.

"Cleton Morse."

Arco grumbled at the sound of his name.

"No middle name, boy? Your parents hate you or something, giving you a name like Cleton with no middle name to make up for it?"

Arco sat quietly, but I could hear the anger in his silence.

"Jennifer Baines McCormick."

"Jenna," she replied.

The officer offered her a smile.

"Jenna it is," he said. "And what's your name, son?"

I responded and heard the snickering of the three drunken teenagers at the strangeness of my name. The officer turned toward the three.

"Now Carl you behave yourself. Purcevil and Cleton, you have no room to mock. Hush up."

P. Roy and Arco visibly flinched.

"Now," said the officer, "what exactly do we have here? Looks like a weenie roast, but I don't see any weenies. Could be a beer bash but only three of you are drunk and those three are all under age. Anyone want to tell me why I'm at a weenie roast at two o'clock in the mornin' and the only weenies I see are drunk?"

The three teenagers kept silent. I clenched my teeth wanting so badly to describe the situation but I felt that I didn't have much credibility with the officer since I could not properly identify myself.

It was Jenna who finally spoke up.

"Tory and I were camping for the night. We were sound asleep when these three *boys* decided to make themselves at home. The big one thought I must look like one of his girlfriends, but I think I'm a lot prettier than the sheep he's used to."

I clenched my teeth to keep from laughing. God she had such a way with words! The office gave her comment a duly earned chuckle and even Trip let out a brief giggle that was quickly stifled by an icy glare from Arco.

"They assaulted my friend here," she continued, "and then Cleton decided he would take advantage of me in my sleep."

The officer listened to Jenna's accounting of what happened. He was silent for a minute and then turned toward the other three.

"You boys agree with what she's tellin' me? Seems only fair to give you a chance to rebut her accusations."

The three cretins looked at each other probably hoping one of the others would say something. The officer waited for a few minutes and then interrupted any train of thought that might have begun.

"Well, I suppose if you had anything to say you would have said it right off. I guess anything you have to say at this point will be a lie, so don't say anything at all."

Then he turned toward me.

"Vagrancy is frowned upon in these parts, Mr. McLeod. You got any money on you so I can pretend that you're just a hiker on his way through?"

I patted my pockets pretending to look for money I knew I didn't have. But when I patted my back pockets, I felt something unfamiliar in one of them. I reached in and found myself holding a neatly folded wad of bills totaling nearly $100. Harlan, or Dorlene, must have slipped it into my pocket when I left!

I held out the cash trying to divert his focus so that he wouldn't see the surprise on my face. Jenna *did* see it and offered her own diversion.

"He's an artist. We're on our way to California."

"Artist?" The officer said. "Like a painter or one of those musical types?"

"Both, sort of," I replied, although the only painting I had ever done involved a house or a barn.

"Well," he continued, "what am I going to do with these rascals? We can take them in and charge them with public intoxication, driving while under the influence and probably get a couple of assault charges thrown in. That should put them square in jail. Miss McCormick, what would you like me to do?"

Arco stared at his feet, waiting for his sentence. Trip began to sob, pleading with Jenna to not press charges. P. Roy looked sick. His eyes floated in their sockets and his jaw hung slack. Then he made the decision for all of them – he threw up.

The stream of vomit landed on the dwindling campfire, dousing it and the light. In the ensuing darkness we heard Arco and Trip scramble toward the truck with a dizzy P. Roy Granger on their heels. The officer made no attempt to chase after the three but instead shone his flashlight on the trail to the road so that P. Roy wouldn't trip and smash his idiot face into the ground.

"You boys behave yourselves and go right home!" He shouted after the three scoundrels then turned back towards us.

"Well don't that beat all? If that boy had puked on my suit or shoes, I would have arrested him on the spot. Besides, I'll be seeing them again tomorrow when they come to collect their ID."

"You all right?" He asked Jenna.

"Yeah. I've got a pretty good defense mechanism. I think I surprised the hell out of them. I think we both did."

"Thank you for showing up when you did," I said.

"Well," he replied, "I guess we should all get out of here. Can't have you sleepin' out here smellin' puke all night. Nothin' worse than the smell of cold beer puke if you ask me."

Jenna and I rolled up our belongings and followed the officer to his car. I sat in the back seat and was delighted that Jenna joined me, rather than sitting up front with the man.

"My name's Jimmy Bolton," he said as he climbed into the driver's seat. "Your names are what again? Jenny and Toby?"

"Jenna and Tory," she corrected.

"Right. Well, where to folks? I guess with a roll of cash like that y'all should be sleepin' in a motel rather than beside the road. I can drop you off at the Homespun closer to Salina if you like."

"That would be fine," I said. "Thank you again."

Jimmy nodded and then turned the car onto the road and sped north.

On the trip to the Homespun, I asked him where he was from. I was not surprised to hear that he was born and raised not too far from Columbia, where I was born and raised. He said that he had fallen in love with a Kansas girl while in school studying Criminal Justice. He married her and then returned to her hometown to set up housekeeping. I told Jimmy that I was also from Columbia and we reminisced about home for a bit.

"I guess you could say that karma put us two Carolina boys on the same road tonight, if you believe in that sort of thing. Good karma, that is. I've had my share of bad karma. Hell, sometimes it feels like my karma ran over my dogma! That's a little philosophy joke I picked up on TV."

Jenna and I laughed at the joke. Jimmy responded to

our appreciation of the humor and continued to make wisecracks all the way to Salina. Eventually, we got to the motel. Jimmy pulled up and got out with us.

"I'm gonna go talk to Josh Barlow, the night manager for a minute. Why don't y'all relax here? Get a Coke from the machine or something."

Jenna scrounged some loose change from the tips she'd collected at Barb O's and bought us both a cold soda. We sat in silence, watching while Jimmy and Joshua chatted inside the manager's office. Periodically they would look out in our direction and Jimmy would throw his winning smile our way. After a few minutes he returned and tossed me a key.

"I told Joshua y'all were needin' a roof and a locked door to keep out the riffraff. I figure y'all can stand to keep as much of that money as you can and since it's so late and he ain't makin' any money tonight anyway he's agreed to let you stay free of charge."

We thanked him profusely and waved to Joshua. Jimmy said he had to head out and patrol the roads for other fellow Southerners being tormented by the local trash.

"Y'all were a great audience," he said. "I haven't had such a good laugh in a long time."

"You missed your calling, Jimmy Bolton." Jenna said, planting a chaste but meaningful kiss on his cheek.

Jimmy blushed a bit, shook my hand, threw one last wave to Joshua and then climbed back into his cruiser. While I said a few final goodbyes and a few more *thank yous*, Jenna went into the manager's office and personally thanked Joshua for the hospitality.

Jimmy finally pulled back onto the highway and disappeared into the night.

As I walked into the manager's office to give my own thanks to Joshua, I heard Jenna chatting it up as she was so good at doing, and knew that we were back to the story that first surfaced at Barb O's.

"...the Elvis Chapel in Vegas. It's kind of a dream of ours. Isn't that right, Tory?"

"Right as rain, sweets."

Jenna brightened at my use of the word "sweets."

"Well, you kids look worn out so I'll let you go get some sleep. Damned shame you ran into those boys. Good thing Jimmy came by. He's a good sort for an Easterner."

I added my own thanks to Jenna's and the two of us left for the room.

I let Jenna have the entire bed as I had been sleeping on the ground and floors for so long that I doubted I would be comfortable on anything soft. She hopped off to the bathroom to have a shower before bed while I curled up on my old reliable blanket on the floor. I was asleep long before she left the shower and the next thing I noticed was the sun peeking through the slats of the Venetian blinds. Despite the ache in my bones and the drowsiness in my eyes, I knew that I would not return to sleep so I rose and went outside to greet the morning.

Interlude
Officer Jimmy Bolton

June 20, 1994
Dear Mr. McCormick,

    I received your letter of June 3rd. Please accept my condolences at the loss of your daughter. I didn't spend much time with her but I do recall her being a sweet girl with a great sense of humor.

    As for Tory, although I can't do much from an official capacity to help locate him, I can tell you that I have not seen him since that night last year. Truth be told, I'm not even sure I would recognize him if I did. We see a hundred or so vagrants through our offices every year so the faces all start to blur after a while. If it wasn't for the fact that Tory left behind a drawing of me, I might not remember him at all.

    You may want to check with Josh Barlow, owner of the Homespun Motel. His information is on the enclosed card. He goes by the name of "Woody" around here. He let them work off their overnight stay up at his place. The kids may have given him a better idea of what their plans were. I will keep an eye out for the boy but unless he looks up Woody or me, we may not even know if he passes through again.

    Again, please accept my deepest sympathy for your loss.

    Sincerely,
    Jimmy Bolton

Continuation
On the Road Again

March 18 – Cincinnati, OH

On the road again. I decided I would like to see Graceland again. Thinking of Elvis will always make me think of Jenna. I picked up a couple of days of "spring cleaning" work so I've got enough cash to get me there. Now back to the story.

Another glorious day rose over the Kansas plains. Just as it had been the day before at Barb O's, the light was perfect for sketching. A note had been tacked to the door inviting us for breakfast at Joshua's house. On the flip side of the note was a map guiding us from the motel to his place, a mile or so up the road. The kindness of the man was genuine and I felt the need to express my appreciation so I returned to the room and retrieved my pad and pencils. I found a stump across the street from the Homespun Motel and began working.

When I returned to the room, satisfied with the Maestro's efforts, Jenna was still sleeping, curled up tight in the fetal position. Her breathing was steady but deep so I knew that she was far from waking. I took the opportunity to have a long, hot shower and wash off as much of the road as I could. It was fabulous and I let the water run until it turned cold.

When I left the bathroom, Jenna was awake and running a brush through her long hair. I secretly wished

I could hold that brush and run it over her beautiful head. She must have heard my thoughts, and I'll tell you that looking back now, I'm convinced she could, because she held the brush out and invited me to finish it for her. As I ran the brush through her hair, I couldn't help but reach up with my free hand and glide my fingers through it. I thought back to the night before when she told me not to fall in love with her and realized that her warning had come too late.

As I slid my hand through her hair my fingers lightly grazed her cheek. I felt her shiver and then pull away slightly. My stomach knotted and my heart ached when she did that. I was suddenly afraid that she did not have the same feelings for me as I did for her. I scolded myself for assuming that she was as attracted to me as I was to her. I decided to keep my mouth shut about my feelings, fearing that expressing them might drive her away. My reaction to her withdrawal must have been obvious as she suddenly leaned back into me, resting her head on my chest.

"Oh, Tory. I'm sorry. Don't take my reaction the wrong way. I wasn't pulling away from you. It's just when your hand touched my face...I felt the same thing when we were dancing the other night."

I didn't understand and told her so. If there was mutual pleasure why did she hide from it? She turned and faced me, insisting that I look into her eyes as she spoke.

"When Arco attacked me last night, I yelled out at him. Do you remember what I yelled?"

I did remember and felt something in my heart give

out.

"Tory, I did not say that to protect myself. I said it to protect him. It was no joke. I have HIV, Tory – the kind that leads to AIDS. That's why I wanted you to promise that you wouldn't fall in love with me. But, I see that it's too late, for both of us."

I sat in silence. She waited patiently. I didn't know what to say. I didn't know how to verbalize the emotions that I felt. I had only known this girl for two days and had fallen so far, so fast, that it couldn't be anything other than destiny. She and I were undeniably connected somehow, possibly even soul mates, and now I was presented with the inevitability of our separation.

I stood up and walked toward the wall, feeling her eyes follow me. I opened my sketchbook and looked down on the two drawings, one of the motel with a phantom shape of Joshua behind the office window, the other of a smiling Officer Jimmy Bolton. My eyes strayed from the drawings to the neck of my wise and trusty friend, Erik.

Carpe diem, Erik said to me. Seize the day.

With all that happened in the past two days, I had lost sight of that message. As I fell deeper and deeper in love with Jenna, I stopped thinking about now and had begun thinking about *tomorrow*. Erik reminded me of the need to live each day to its fullest. I had been given an opportunity to meet my destiny and I wasn't going to let it slip by. I knew that I had to make the most out of my time with Jenna – every single minute we had together. It frightened me a little to think that so much could change in so little time. It was as if my entire life had suddenly and permanently changed course.

I turned to Jenna and offered a smile through a trickle of tears.

"I suppose then the only thing to do now is to find a Laundromat!"

Jenna stared at me in disbelief.

"Did you hear me, Tory? Anything I said?"

"You're falling in love with me," I replied. "Which is good. It makes falling in love with you so much easier, although it wasn't much of a struggle on its own."

"Is that all?"

"You have HIV."

"Yes."

"The one that leads to AIDS."

"Yes."

"Which means that if we're going to fall in love, we have to enjoy every second we have together. I say we start at the Laundromat. My clothes could use a scrub and I think yours could too."

Jenna shook her head and a faint smile crossed her lips.

"Ok," she said, and rose off the bed to collect her things.

As we packed up our meager belongings, I asked Jenna how she had contracted the virus. I suppose declaring your love for someone makes it easier to ask personal questions, as I didn't hesitate to find out more about her condition.

Jenna told me about the car accident when she was sixteen, and the transfusion that introduced the HIV virus to her system. She assured me, over and over, despite my pledge that I believed her, that she had not contracted the condition through sex or drug use. It seemed important to her that I trust in her virtue. I did. I still do.

As we left the room, Jenna snatched Joshua's note from the door. We decided to stop by his house before going on to the laundry. Before we left, we stopped in the motel office and left the drawing with the day manager, Gloria. She agreed to give the picture to Joshua when he came in. Jenna thought it would be a nice surprise for him rather than to take it directly to his house.

The directions Joshua left to his house were excellent and we were soon standing on his front porch ringing the bell. A tall, narrow woman in her early thirties answered the door wiping her hands on a kitchen towel. She looked at us with a bit of hesitation but then her face changed as if she recognized us.

"Tory and Jenna?" She asked.

"Yes, Ma'am." Jenna and I replied in concert.

"I'm Ruth," the woman said, thrusting out a hand in greeting.

"Woody told me you might be coming but I thought you might be traveling Bible thumpers for a minute. Come on in."

We were soon to learn that Joshua preferred to be called Woody, although I never did find out why.

We entered the house, which was furnished with antiques and rural artifacts. Jenna followed Ruth down the long hallway while I stowed our rucksacks in a side room.

I wandered down the hallway in the direction they had taken, looking at the pictures on the walls as I walked. Many of them were pictures of a younger Woody in a baseball uniform, posing with a bat, a glove and ball – the usual baseball photos. The name across the front of the Jersey read, "Toledo." I'm not much of a baseball follower but I knew that there wasn't a major league team in Toledo. I thought maybe I would ask Woody about the pictures but unfortunately never got around to it.

As I turned through a door leading into an enormous kitchen, I was struck full force by the excruciatingly delicious scent of pancakes, eggs, and sausage. The combination of those aromas blended and I thought of my mother's kitchen on Saturdays when the same delicious perfume filled the air. I was overwhelmed by a sudden sense of nostalgia and loss and for a moment I thought I would cry, but the thick, milky voice of Woody brought me back to the present with a warm greeting and invitation to sit next to him.

"It tastes better than it smells, son."

He was right. Breakfast was incredible. Ruth had mastered a way of making scrambled eggs that surpassed any that I had eaten previously. (Garlic, cayenne pepper, and a touch of Cream of Tartar, for whichever of you does the cooking!) The pancakes were home mixed, not from the box. The syrup was also homemade but not maple; rather it was a concoction of butter, brown sugar, and some other mystery ingredient. If left long enough on the plate to cool, the mixture crystallized slightly, effectively candy-coating the hot cakes it covered. The sausage was purchased from a local man and although it was unavoidably greasy, the spices sang on the tongue and mixed perfectly with eggs. Coffee, not as thick as Barb O's but easily as rich, orange juice, tomato juice, but enough! Just describing it makes me want to march back to Woody and Ruth and stuff myself until I explode!

Jenna and I ate as politely as our ravenous stomachs would allow. Ruth and Woody kept pace with us and more than once one or the other got up to fix a new batch of eggs or fry up some more sausage. The conversation raced from topic to topic but always seemed to land back on my travels or Jenna's childhood. Our hosts seemed to be as hungry for our stories as we were for their food. Not a bad trade if you ask me!

When the meal was over, we insisted on cleaning up. There were plates and pans everywhere and when we surveyed the battleground, we both felt a bit guilty for being such gluttons. Still, we did not regret a single drop of syrup or fleck of spice. I washed, Jenna dried, and Woody put the dishes away while Ruth sat at the table leaning on her slender hand, supervising.

It was wonderful. I was struck with a sense of reunion, which is strange considering that I had only recently met all of these people. It was then that I began to realize that family is not so much a matter of genealogy as it is sense of belonging on a spiritual level. What a strange and wonderful world I had stumbled on! With so many miles over the passing years, how could I have been so blind to these sensations? Jenna had called me a catalyst back at Barb O's. I was beginning to think that she belonged in the same category. Sometime a few nights back I had fallen asleep in the same predictable, competitive world I had lived in for 25 years. The next morning I woke up in a new world full of beauty, promise, and irony all interwoven and inseparable. Jenna was the reason for my new vision and understanding.

As I handed each wet plate to Jenna my fingers would brush over hers. Each time we touched our eyes would meet and a silly grin would pass over both our faces. How I wanted to hold her! To touch her face! To kiss her! I wondered if she felt the same desire. I couldn't tell. I can honestly say that my experience with women up until that point was extremely limited. I had only one romantic relationship in my life and that was a major disappointment all around. I was so excited by the things I felt for Jenna that I regretted not making a better effort in the past. Still, I've met thousands of people and none ever touched my heart the way your daughter did.

When the dishes were done and the kitchen returned to its pre-pig out state, Woody took his leave of us. He worked the night shift in the motel, which he owned, as it was difficult to find anyone in the area that would work those hours. Ruth had gotten herself on a similar schedule so that the two could spend time together. Instead of joining him in bed, however, she sat with Jenna and I for a little while longer until her uncontrollable yawning told me it might be best if we left.

"Why don't you two stay here until we get up in a little while?" Ruth offered.

After a few minutes of amiable debate, we agreed to wait for them but insisted on being assigned chores of some kind in payment for our full stomachs and hearts. Ruth laughed and told us that the yard could use some work – mowing, trimming, pruning, weeding, the usual things. We accepted the challenge but I was concerned that the roar of the mower might keep them awake.

Ruth laughed.

"I've been sleeping with the loudest snoring man in three states for the past eight years. And he could sleep through an atomic war. You go right ahead and do what you can. You won't disturb us. Help yourselves to some lunch when you feel the need."

With that she climbed the stairs and we didn't see her until just before dark.

It was still fairly early in the morning and despite Ruth's assurance that she and Woody could sleep through our activities, Jenna and I decided to wait until the afternoon to begin the noisy business of yard work. Instead we took the opportunity to sit by the pond in back of the house and spend some quiet time together. We sat in silence for a long time, watching the fish come up and snap at insects on the surface of the water. Jenna pulled a blade of grass and chewed on the fleshy tip. I laid back and watched the billowy clouds blow over the Kansas sky.

"I feel like I've known you all my life," Jenna said, finally breaking the silence.

"I know what you mean," I replied.

"Weird, huh?"

"Yes," I said, "but it feels right."

Jenna lay down next to me. Her long hair billowed around her head, some of it brushing against my cheek. I continued to watch the clouds. At one point I turned to offer a question to Jenna and found her looking at me, smiling. The question left my mind before it could find my mouth. To this day I can't remember what it was I wanted to ask.

"I was looking at your profile," she said.

I was suddenly self-conscious, something I had not been since the day I set out on the road. Another change in my life brought on by your exquisite daughter!

"I'd like to kiss you," she said, softly. "May I?"

I was suddenly very nervous and for a variety of reasons. First, I had minimal experience in the field of romance, and it had been a long time since I had kissed or been kissed in such a manner. Second, her ability to almost read my thoughts and express them before I had a chance to hide them was very unsettling. Third, I knew enough about HIV to know that it was a highly contagious virus that passed through body fluids. (One of my many trips to the library!) At that time I wasn't sure if saliva counted and what I didn't know was far scarier than what I did. Nevertheless, my response was short and to the point.

"Yes."

Jenna leaned over on her elbow and slowly brushed her lips across mine. I must have seemed like a statue. I didn't know if I should respond and simply lay there with my eyes closed, receiving her gift. Then quite suddenly, her lips left mine and her kiss found my cheek. I opened my eyes and looked into hers. She was smiling but a tear had formed and was making its slow course down her cheek. I was lost. Hopelessly, irretrievably lost.

Jenna returned to her reclining position, only now with her head resting on my chest. We watched the clouds together for a few minutes. She chewed on another blade of grass, while I ran my fingers through her long, blonde hair.

"Are you afraid of death, Tory?" She asked suddenly.

I hadn't thought about it before and told her so. She asked me to take a few minutes and think about it. The few minutes passed without any kind of enlightenment so I told her that I'm not exactly afraid of it but it wasn't something I thought about enough to really develop a philosophy for it.

"I'm not afraid of death," she said. "Though, I am afraid of dying. I don't want to die in agony or waste away over an extended period of time. I want it to be quick and painless. Then I think I can appreciate the beauty of it. Is that crazy?"

I told her I thought it was extremely sane to be so conscious of an unknown inevitability that you were sure there is bound to be beauty in it. The silence returned and we enjoyed the warming of the day.

The yard work went quickly as there were only a few small patches of grass that could be diplomatically called *lawn* to mow. Jenna knelt down in Ruth's garden plucking weeds like a pro. We were done and quite sweaty by 3:00pm so we decided to take our chances and test out the pond.

I peeled off my sweat soaked shirt and shoes and walked into the water until it was about neck deep. The bottom was soft, with very few rocks so it was easy on the feet.

I heard a splash behind me and felt the swell of the water as Jenna jumped in rather than waded as I had. I turned to make a comment regarding her wild entrance and felt the words freeze in my mouth as I saw her clothes – all of them – in a pile next to my shirt and shoes. She had stripped off every stitch and was now in the water as naked as the day she was born. With me!

"Close your mouth, Tory McLeod," she giggled. "You're liable to catch flies!"

I snapped my jaw shut and tried to remove the idiot expression from my face. I didn't know what to say. Her boldness continued to amaze me.

"Something to check off my list," she said as she swam over to where I was standing neck deep.

"Your list?"

"I didn't tell you about my list? Well, I'll have to sometime."

"Why not now?" I asked, hoping to divert my mind from the fact that the woman I was falling in love with was so close by wearing nothing but her own beauty.

She laughed, as she continued to swim circles around me, causing me to slowly turn in place in order to keep her in sight. I wasn't trying to ogle her. The dark water kept her modestly covered. I was simply trying to appear nonchalant, as if her behavior had not shocked me so much.

"I have a list of things I want to do before…Well,

you know."

"Like what?" I asked.

"Oh, ride a motorcycle, eat caviar, yodel from the top of a mountain, sing in a nightclub, that sort of thing. I keep the list in my journal and check each thing off as I do them."

"So what do you get to check off this time?" I asked.

"Skinny-dipping in broad daylight. Although I modified that one last night along with a number of others."

"Modified?"

"Yeah," she said, ducking completely under the water and surfacing only a couple of feet away from me.

"Skinny-dipping in broad daylight…with Tory."

She punctuated her statement by quickly splashing away from me causing me to turn my head from the spray of water. When she had moved far enough away, I turned back.

"How many things are on your list?" I asked.

"I don't know. A hundred, maybe more."

"How many have you accomplished?"

"So far?"

"Yes."

"One."

She disappeared under the water again and surfaced several yards away.

"Only one?" I asked. "Why only one?"

"Well, I've only just begun keeping track."

By this time I had been sufficiently distracted from the fact that she was naked beneath the pond's surface. I was extremely interested in this list and thought it was something I might try myself.

I realized that time was on my side and it would not be so amazing a feat to accomplish my goals as it would be for someone whose time was questionable and undoubtedly short – like Jenna.

"What else is on the list?" I asked.

I was intrigued by the concept and in love with the sound of her voice as she splashed about and listed the variety of goals she had set for herself. But something was missing from her list and without thinking I asked.

"What about making love in some unique place?"

I realized my mistake almost immediately after the words left my lips. Jenna stopped splashing and stared at me.

"That's not funny," she said and swam to the edge of the pond. I turned away from her in respect for her modesty as much as in shame for my carelessness. I searched for an apology. I kicked myself for being so caught up in the moment that I forgot the reason she had compiled the list in the first place. I had never before, and never since, felt so stupid.

After a time I turned to see if she was dressed. She was gone, as were her clothes, and I was suddenly afraid that she would leave. I scrambled from the water and grabbed my shirt and shoes as I ran toward the house hoping that I would be able to stop her if that was what she had in mind. I ran through a litany of apologies in my head but none were sufficient. All fell short of what I truly felt.

As I rounded the corner of the house into the front yard I saw Jenna sitting on the porch swing, towel drying her hair. I slowed my pace and approached with great caution and immeasurable humility.

"Jenna, I..."

"Come up here and see this," she said, her tone once again light as if my stupid remark in the pond had never happened.

I climbed onto the porch and sat next to her on the swing. She handed me a small book with a cover resembling green marble. I opened it and saw the words, "A Written Collection of My Things, by Jennifer Baines McCormick" written across the title page.

"Read on McLeod," she said.

I scanned the first few pages, each laden with words written across a variety of angles. The margins were full. The lines between the lines were full. Her journal was more than a collection. It was a bird's nest of thoughts and observations. I stopped on a page and read everything she had written. Such thoughts had never crossed my mind and I felt like a paper philosopher compared to the completeness of the wit and ideas Jenna had captured. Near the middle of the book I found her "To Do" list. It covered several pages spanning goals as spontaneously derived, as they were ordered and logical.

On the third page of the list I found the entry she had referred to earlier, *Skinny-dipping in broad daylight* and then an annotation in another color of ink, *with Tory!* This entry, unlike all of the others, had a line drawn through it. I thumbed through the remaining pages until I reached the end of the list. There at the bottom was what was surely a new entry – *Make love*.

I closed the book and turned to say something but my

mouth closed around emptiness and I returned my gaze to the marbled green cover of the book. The silence that followed was unbearable but I could not seem to collect enough of a thought or put together the right words to tell her how I felt. I wanted to touch her. To hold her. To tell her how sorry I was for being so insensitive but I felt that any attempt I made would not be acceptable for the careless remark I made.

I felt a tap on my shoulder and turned to see Jenna holding out her hairbrush. I took it and put it to use. She settled back into me, making it difficult for me to properly brush out her hair, but I didn't mind. The closeness and contact were intoxicating. I was drunk with her presence. When I reached the point where I could no longer stand the guilt of my comment while feeling the warmth of her next to me, I dropped the brush and wrapped my arms around her, pulling her closer until my face rested in the bed of her neck.

"I'm so stupid," I said.

Jenna responded by hugging the arms that hugged her so tightly.

"Hush," she whispered. "You were right. That is something I want to do before…you know. I had just convinced myself that it would not happen. That it could not happen. Now I want it more than ever and I'm afraid."

I remained silent, thinking that she was between thoughts. I held her closer and closer until I felt I would pull her right into me. I wanted to know if she wanted this thing with me, but I couldn't ask.

"With you," she whispered, her lips brushing against

my temple.

The creak of the screen door behind us startled us from our embrace. Woody walked out onto the porch, stretching widely. His back responded with several audible snaps and pops.

"Still here?"

"Yes," I replied. "We wanted to repay you for your kindness and that incredible breakfast so Ruth set us to some yard work."

"I see," he said, scanning the front yard, nodding his approval.

"Nice job. Why are you all wet?"

"We took a swim in the pond," Jenna answered.

"By the looks of it, one of you forgot that skinny dippin' means takin' your clothes off!"

"Gotta get him to loosen up!" Jenna laughed.

"I should say so. Ruthie and I go out dippin' on those really hot summer nights. Never went out during the day, though, not that there's anyone around to see us if we did."

Woody stretched again and the few joints that hadn't cracked the first time made sure to join in for the second chorus.

"Well, y'all could probably use a shower after splashin' about in that mud hole. I see you know where the towels are so make yourselves at home and wash off the algae and fish turds. I'll get Ruthie up and see what we can throw together to eat."

Jenna took my hand and led me into the house. She pulled a thick towel down from the shelf in the linen closet and guided me to the bathroom.

We stood there in the doorway of the bathroom for a few minutes, just looking at each other. I was still feeling pangs of guilt for my stupidity, but her smile put me somewhat at ease. A surge of confidence ran through me and I indicated with a nod of my head that she was welcome to join me in the shower. She smiled and blushed a little but declined.

"Not yet," she said, then turned and walked back to the kitchen.

March 19 – Still in Cincinnati, OH

Sorry.
I had to stop and think about what I had written and what was coming up. I'm struggling a bit with this but I think I need to tell it all to put it in perspective for you. I realized that telling you all of these intimate things about your daughter might not be in the best taste. I hope you don't think me some kind of opportunist. I was simply responding to an incredible sense of physical and spiritual attraction, something I had never felt before.

I believe that Jenna and I were meant for each other, if you'll pardon the cliché. I fell in love with her emotionally and spiritually first. The physical love came later. All combined made me feel whole, more than I had ever felt before or since. If something I describe upsets or offends you, I apologize. I don't blame you if you tear out those pages or even throw this notebook in the fireplace. But, I hope you'll continue. It would mean so much to her for you to know us as we were when we were together.

We spent the rest of the afternoon with Woody and Ruth until it was nearly 7:00pm and Woody had to go run the motel. Ruth invited us to stay but I felt the need to be moving on. This time Jenna would be going with me and I was excited in expectation of the time we would spend together.

Jenna and I cleaned up the dinner dishes and then packed up our gear. It was then that I remembered the sketch of Officer Bolton and asked Woody if he would see that the picture was delivered. He agreed, and with a final hug for Ruth we piled into Woody's pick-up truck and rolled away.

Woody took us ten miles past the far Western edge of Salina before dropping us off. We made our goodbyes and then he was gone, rumbling back down the highway toward the Homespun Motel. I told Jenna that I hoped he and Ruth liked the drawing. She said that I should consider doing something up for Ruth and mailing it to her from somewhere down the road.

And so we were off, traveling the highways of the Midwest across the pancake plains of Central and Eastern Kansas on our way to California. Three days I had known her – three days! But I felt as if I was traveling with a life-long companion. Even more that that. She felt like someone I had known for many lifetimes, if you believe in that sort of thing, which I do. There was far too much connection and continuity in our relationship to be forged in so short a time. She was far too capable of picking up on my feelings and thoughts, although I struggled to find the same psychic connection to her. It had to be destiny. But just as I knew that she and I were joined for a reason, I also sensed that she and I would soon be parted. But as Erik would say, "Carpe Diem!"

We stopped in a small town off the main highway

and bought some supplies at an all-night convenience store with the money given to me by Harlan (or Dorlene). I looked for a Laundromat but could not find one open late. We decided to camp outside the town and do our cleaning in the morning.

We found an open field and set up our meager camp. We had an unobstructed view of the universe and throughout our late meal we found ourselves looking up at the dazzling display of stars. I pointed out the major constellations, many of which Jenna already knew, and told her stories associated with each. I also pointed out some of the lesser-known groups and told her stories about some of those as well.

Jenna listened to my ramblings, genuinely interested it seemed. I was actually amazed to discover just how much I knew about the sky, as I had never had an opportunity to regurgitate my knowledge.

It was great!

Sometime after midnight we fell asleep on our respective bedrolls. The night was warm and clear and I thought as I drifted toward dreamland that it was probably the best day I'd had in a very long time.

The laundry was an event. Many of the machines in this town were broken and took our quarters without so much as a drop of water or a thank you! I'm embarrassed to say that it had been a few weeks since my clothes had been properly cleaned. I try to wash them each week, but often my only resource is a back yard spigot and a bar of soap. I do my best with what I have, but sometimes it isn't enough. So, I ran my clothes through the wash twice before feeling relatively confident they were cleansed of the past weeks of dirt, dust, and downpour.

We talked a great deal while the loads were running. I asked about her list and how serious she was at accomplishing those things. She said that up until that previous day it was just a list but now it was a challenge. I told her that I would help her in any way I could although with my pitiful resources, I seriously doubted my ability to offer anything.

Jenna asked about Erik and I told her all that I've told you and she seemed amused and intrigued that I had such a relationship with a musical instrument.

"Play something for me," she said.

Other than the two of us, the Laundromat was empty so I unwrapped Erik from the plastic sheet that served as his raincoat and tuned him up. After a quick check of the strings, a few strums across the basic chords, I began a fair rendition of Bob Seger's *Night Moves*. Jenna sat with her arms wrapped around her knees, her eyes closed and her head moving with the music. Her long blonde hair swayed with the melody, hypnotically relieving my slight case of stage fright, and allowing the Maestro to come forth and perform.

I suppose I should explain this "Maestro" business to you as I have referred to him several times now and have never gotten around to explaining what I'm talking about. Of course, doing this now may seem like an interruption but if I don't do it now, while I'm thinking about it, I probably won't get to it and you'll read this letter thinking I'm schizophrenic or something.

When I create something, whether it's music, poetry,

or a drawing, I go into a sort of trance and my consciousness retreats into the background. What comes forward is an entity capable of capturing a moment in a song, verse, or image – something that doesn't seem to happen when I consciously try to do these things. I call this entity the Maestro, as he is the one with the talent – the one that sees the truth in things, the beauty in things. He is a part of me, but he operates on his own terms and quite separately from the rest of me. (Except my body of course.) He has the eyes, the ear, and the voice to express what I feel deep within. So when you read these references to this other *me*, it is that spirit which I refer to. And now back to your regularly scheduled broadcast!

After a few songs, Jenna insisted that I sing something of my own. She knew from our previous conversations that I had several original songs in my repertoire, and wanted to hear what the Maestro had done. Since the alternate *me* was still near the surface, I broke into one of my more recent numbers, *Buyin' Time*. The tune is depressing and the lyrics morose but before I could think about something more upbeat, I was already at the first chorus.

> *The road is longer than my life. (Buyin' time. Buyin' time)*
> *It's paved with loneliness and strife. (Buyin' time. Buyin' time)*
> *Far more walkin' than I've got livin'.*
> *Leavin' Hell and lookin' for Heaven.*
> *Buyin' time, from day to day,*
> *Don't have a dime, no one to pay.*

I think you can get the gist of the song by that snippet of lyrics. But, despite the sullen message, Jenna enjoyed it.

"Why are you on the road?" She asked. "Why aren't you performing professionally? Or selling your songs, or art?"

I had heard these questions a hundred times before and until that day, it never really mattered to me if the person posing the question knew why or not, so I usually dodged the question. But, I wanted her to know.

"I'm a little afraid of failure," I confessed after a few moments of contemplation.

"Failure?" She laughed. "For crying out loud, Tory, you could sell dirt to a farmer and you know it! What makes you think you couldn't sell something of value, like your talent?"

I had no response to that. My pat answer had always been something evasive like, "I am doing it professionally. I get paid in food or lodging for what I do." I knew that was bull and also knew that Jenna would see through it as well, but just as I didn't pry into other people's personal affairs, I protected my own. Until I met Jenna, that is. I wanted her to know everything about me, including my insecurities. For the first time in years I was actually putting myself in line for criticism and I didn't doubt Jenna's ability to dish it out.

Jenna must have sensed my reaction to her comments and let up on the pressure. Behind her a washing machine buzzed indicating that her clothes were clean.

"Just something to think about," she said, stroking my arm with her narrow hand. "For your future. Play me something else while I put these in the dryer."

I stared at the guitar strings for a minute or so and then broke into a modified version of *Obla Di Obla Da*, replacing the name "Desmond" with "Jenna" and "Molly" with "Tory." Jenna laughed when she heard what I had done and sang the chorus along with me while she danced around the washing machines. When the lyrics got to the exclamation *Bra!*, Jenna held up that particular part of her wardrobe and swung it around her head, inciting hoots of laughter from both of us. The Maestro had retreated and all that was left was plain old Tory, singing and goofing around with this miracle of a woman.

With the laundry done and packed in our respective rucksacks, we made our way back to the highway and continued our journey to California.

March 20 – Somewhere in Kentucky

Looking back through what I have already written, I see that I have spent a great deal of time describing our first few days together. What an incredibly long letter this will be if I continue to be so verbose! I decided to take a break and figure out how I can economize my words without omitting anything that may be of interest to you. I'll make my best attempt but please forgive me for determining what is and isn't interesting to you.

We began our hike west. The straight, flat geometry of the Kansas roadways made the walk easy. We kept to the secondaries but chose not to hitchhike, as we wanted to spend the time together. We passed enormous fields of wheat that stretched on to the horizons. We crossed several small streams, many of them more likely irrigation ditches, which offered a break in the miles of identical highway.
We had acquired enough supplies back in that small town at the eastern edge of this no-man's land to last us several days. I figured we could make it all week with what we carried between us and that should get us to the Colorado border. We still had some money left over, enough to eat light until we made it to Denver. After that we would have to work to earn our meals. I was

concerned about the effects of nutrition of Jenna's condition so I made sure she ate everything we prepared and even feigned a stomachache or two to allow her the opportunity to clean up my leftovers.

But I'm generalizing and I'm doing it far ahead of the point where I left off!

Our second day on the road provided us one of the few real pleasures, in my opinion, of living in such a flat region. Way off in the distance, across the miles of prairie grass, a storm was brewing.

We sat beside the road and watched nature's fireworks flash and spark as the thunderstorm rolled uncontested across the prairie. Our own sky was clear and blue and the sun shone down on us, darkening our skin. The thunderhead moved slowly, almost imperceptibly, and the lightning danced across the clouds and the ground. It was spectacular!

We held hands while we observed this natural display of power, feeling a bit sorry for those caught in the path of that fury. Our sympathy would have been much deeper had we known then that the very next day we would be facing the same ferocity ourselves!

I was awakened in the morning, as I am every morning, not by the sun but by the dawn itself. Had the sun been my only alarm clock, I would have slept well past three in the afternoon, as it wasn't until much later in the day that we saw the fingers of light poke through the thick clouds.

The morning that greeted us was so dark that I had to check Jenna's watch to see if it was in fact morning. The storm clouds pitched and rolled above us, utterly blocking out the rising sun.

I roused Jenna and told her that we had to get moving as quickly as possible to find shelter from the impending storm. When she saw the roiling clouds, she scrambled like a well-trained Marine. We knew that there was no shelter behind us and nothing in sight to the north or south of the highway, so we moved swiftly down the road into the heart of the monster, hoping to find a refuge before it unleashed its fury on us. We were not so lucky.

The wind picked up as we pressed on and was soon buffeting us with heavy gusts. Within an hour, the rain began spattering us with enormous drops of a truly primed thunderstorm. Although it was far from a downpour, more of a light shower by meteorological standards, the drops were so dense with water that we were quickly drenched.

We pressed on, quickening our pace, and crossed from open prairie to neatly farmed land. Jenna shouted that there must be a house or a barn nearby. I agreed but also pointed out that this far into the heartland the farms were enormous and the home of the owner might be miles off the highway. As we had no idea which direction to go to find either, we pressed on.

A few trees, thick with leaves, offered a tempting umbrella from the rain and wind, but despite the attractiveness of dry ground, the fear of a lightning strike kept us away. And lightning did strike!

I caught a whiff of ozone just as the first of a volley of earsplitting crashes accompanied a finger of brilliant light that struck, and split, one of the telephone poles that lined the highway. The strike was so close to us that we were both plagued with the ghostly trail of the lightning across our eyes as well as a shrill ringing brought on by the thunder. Jenna shrieked and began running down the road. I followed, moving as quickly as my rucksack and Erik would allow.

Then the hail fell.

I had heard of baseball-sized hail before, but until that day the biggest I had seen was about the size of a large grape. Fortunately the shower was not dense so we managed to move quite effectively without getting hit by any of the icy fastballs. Ahead of us in the gloom was a wide ditch crossed by a short bridge. As we approached, I saw that the ditch was not very deep and that we would be able to climb underneath the bridge to escape the next inning. I shouted to Jenna to duck under the bridge but she had already come upon the same idea and was nearly under before I stopped shouting.

It was dark beneath the bridge, but a muddy light found its way underneath, enabling us to find a dry place to sit. Jenna plopped down and began wiggling her fingers in her ears, presumably trying to rid herself of the same incessant ringing that I was also hearing. In the darkness under the bridge, I could still see the ghost of the thunderbolt. We had narrowly escaped being incinerated by lightning, and pummeled by the Nolan Ryan of the skies. The bridge was a welcome haven from the tempest that was only beginning to gather itself all around us.

"There," Jenna said, opening her jaw widely. "Finally got them to pop. Wasn't that great?"

I laughed. She had shrieked like a B movie scream

queen when the lightning and hail began. Now she was ready for more. The world had become an amusement park to her. Every experience just another trip on the roller coaster or another chance to knock all the bottles down and win a stuffed bear. I envied her vision.

"Come here," she said. Rising, she took my arm and pulled me next to her. "Open up your pack and get out some clothes. You need to get out of these wet ones."

I was a bit embarrassed when she pulled at the tail of my shirt and then lifted it over my head. She spread the shirt out over the dry ground beneath the bridge. She turned and saw me watching her and smiled. Above us the rain came hard, drumming on the bridge and adding to the stream that flowed through the ditch. Jenna stood silhouetted by the meager light from the world beyond the bridge. Behind her, the rain fell in torrents, but I could not see beyond the shadowy figure in front of me as she too lifted her drenched shirt above her head, then dropping it, walked toward me and wrapped her arms around my waist.

I cannot describe for you what I felt as our skin touched. Partially because you're her parents and I am a lot more than a little embarrassed to describe it. Mostly because the words have not been invented yet. If I could speak a hundred languages – a thousand! – I could not describe that sensation. It can only be known by those who have truly known love.

Time on the road is longer than time in normal life. Without the distractions of work and family and friends, with only miles of road and the search for the next meal, or a warm dry place to camp, one can invest their full energy into the analysis of a single thought. I had thought about this moment solidly for the past few days. I had followed each thread of possibility as far as logic would allow and I was aware of the risks as well as the rewards.

Jenna leaned up and kissed me softly. She moved to speak, but I stopped her with a touch of my fingers on her lips.

"I have been wandering for so long," I said. "I didn't think that I had a goal, but now I know that I do. It is you. It was no coincidence that you were on that porch, or in that pick-up truck with those creeps. It was as pure a symbol of destiny as there could ever be. I love you, Jenna. I love you with a love that began long ago and has only now found the opportunity to be fulfilled. I want to be with you forever and beyond."

Jenna stood silent. Tears rolled down her cheeks and her breath hitched with shallow sobs. She turned and moved away from me.

My empty arms fell like lead weights to my sides.

I committed too soon, I thought.

I felt like an idiot for making such a deeply spiritual pledge without first knowing her own feelings. For the second time since I had known her, I felt as if I had pushed too hard, and in doing so pushed her away. But damn it, I had only spoken the truth!

Jenna opened her bedroll and laid it out in the darkness. All around us the rain crashed down, thundering on the bridge above and swelling the stream. I turned away from her as I did in the pond at Woody's house. Shame and frustration swam through me and I clenched my jaw tightly to fight back the tears that threatened to humble the rain.

"Tory," her voice called from the darkness. "Come."

I turned and saw that she was kneeling on the bedroll, her arms outstretched.

"Come."

I walked slowly to where she knelt and dropped to my knees in front of her. We were both trembling. She took my hands in hers and our shaking seemed to synchronize causing our entwined fingers to vibrate, almost comically, together.

"I love you, too. There are no words to describe what I feel since I've known you. When we're together, whether in moments of playfulness or talking about our dreams or problems or whatever, you never run out of ways to touch my heart. I love you. I can't tell you or show you how much in one lifetime."

We made love until the rain stopped. Not the stiff, clumsy sort one might expect of virgins, because despite my sparse previous experience, I felt as much like a virgin as she was. This was not the tentative exploration of a back seat romance. It wasn't awkward. Instead, we melted together, becoming one entity, loving and evolving, ceasing to be individuals, each motion in balance with the other. The storm raged in concert with our act until we lay exhausted, wrapped in each other's arms, tears streaming down our cheeks, listening to the storm rumble its way across the prairie.

I'm sorry. I have to stop for now.

March 21 – Lexington, KY

Telling you that was difficult. I wanted you to know the power of what we had without getting overly descriptive. How exactly does one tell their in-laws, particularly the father-in-law, about their daughter's first time? Even now, tears pour down my cheeks in memory of those few moments in the cosmic clock where the entire universe came together at a single point under a bridge in Eastern Kansas. It's amazing sometimes where miracles choose to manifest themselves.

The chirping of the birds and the return of the sun brought us back from the fringes of that *otherworld* we had created. Jenna was up first, padding boldly naked to the edge of the protected area to look up into the brilliant blue sky that followed the storm. I rose and dressed in some dry things, then carried her rucksack over to her so she could also dress. As I laid the pack beside her, she turned sharply and hugged my tightly. She was crying.
"Tory, I'm sorry if I hurt you," she cried. "I'm sorry if I killed you. I was stupid. Stupid!"
I held her tightly and stroked her hair, assuring her that whatever price I must pay for what we did was well worth the joy I felt in finding her, and that life without her would not be worth living.

"Let the consequences run their course," I said. "If I am condemned to the same fate you are, so be it. And whether I am to lead or follow across the division between life and death, I will do it knowing that we will be rejoined on the other side."

"Oh, Tory," she cried. "You don't know what you're saying. You're so beautiful and so strong, but you don't know. You can't mean what you're saying."

I meant those words then. I mean them even more now that she's gone.

In the pragmatic, morally structured world we live in, we were fools to undertake that adventure without protection. I suppose I am due a fair scolding by the various AIDS support groups and safe sex advocates. I'm not sure I have contracted the virus. I should probably get tested. But what I did, I did to myself. I did it for love, and not the temporary, physical love of casual sex, but rather the kind of love that poets write about. The kind that carries men through the worst possible hardships. The kind that only God in His many faces and names can give. I have not infected another person. I have not felt any physical desire since the day she passed away.

She is, and always will be, my one and only. So let them scold!

We walked in silence, hands entwined, for several miles, making our way back to the main highway. The storm had cooled the air and the breeze that followed in its wake was refreshing. We chewed on granola bars as we walked, taking in the beauty of the prairie after a vicious summer storm.

I felt strange, at once joyful yet fearful of what the consequences of our lovemaking might be. I had not thought much about death, even when my parents were both killed. Now the reality of it flooded me. If I had contracted the virus, how long did I have before it claimed me? And Jenna! How long for her?

Jenna remained silent. I knew she was thinking about what we had done. The expression on her face was not one of happy remembrance. Her furrowed brow and downcast eyes were more the look of someone puzzling over some elusive problem.

"Are you all right?" I asked more than once.

She only responded by squeezing my hand but didn't once open her mouth to tell me what she was feeling. I began to feel anxious.

She turned suddenly and stuck her thumb out. I had not even heard the approaching car but even in her deep concentration, Jenna had sensed it.

"They'll stop," she said quietly, keeping her gaze on the approaching Jeep.

She was right, of course. They did.

We ran toward the car and stopped by the passenger window.

The driver, a wide-faced man with thick round glasses and thinning hair greeted us with a British accent.

"Salutations, fellow travelers! I see you survived the storm!"

"Greetings!" Jenna replied, her smile erasing the look of concern she had been wearing for miles. "We ducked under a bridge when the big one hit. Good thing, too. It would have ruined my day if one of us had gotten beaned by one of those hail stones!"

"I should say so," the stranger laughed. "Where are you two headed?"

"Vegas," I replied before Jenna had an opportunity. She glanced at me, winked and smiled.

"Well, well! How fortunate for us all! My wife and I are also on our way to the city of Lost Wages. You're welcome to hop in for as long as you like."

We had thought that the man was alone until he mentioned his companion. A woman lay curled up in the back seat, oblivious to our presence let alone the fact that the vehicle had stopped. Jenna climbed into the front leaving me to hop into the back next to the sleeping woman. I carefully laid our packs and Erik in the far back, trying not to wake my snoozing bench mate.

"Denise, darling," the driver called. "We have company!"

He pulled away with such speed that the poor woman was nearly crushed into the back of the seat. I offered a hand and helped her sit up. She thanked me offhandedly, seemingly unconcerned that there were now two strangers in the car.

"Bernie," she said after consciousness settled in, "are you going to introduce me to your friends or what?"

Her accent was as thickly New York-ish as her companion's was British. Although sitting, I could tell she was tall. She had a narrow frame, long red hair and stunning gray-green eyes, a combination that made her exquisitely beautiful but not in a super-model, Barbie doll, way. Her beauty was completely natural and I found it hard not to look at her.

"Well, lovey," Bernie replied as we sped down the highway. "I haven't had the pleasure myself."

Jenna introduced both of us and Bernie reciprocated. (Denise insisted on being called Denny.) Once again we told the story about getting married in the Elvis Chapel. Our hosts were heading the same way but with a brief stop in Vail, Colorado.

"My sister," Denny offered. "I haven't seen her in a few years and since she's practically on the way, we decided to stop for a bit."

"That's great." Jenna said. "I wish I had a sister. I'm an only child."

Of all the topics we had discussed, we had only touched briefly on our families. I knew about you two but wasn't aware until that moment that Jenna was an only child, like me.

"Me too," I said.

"That makes it a trio," Bernie announced, glancing in the rearview mirror. "It seems darling that you are the only one of us blessed with a sibling."

The chatter in the car continued for miles. Each of us told our stories and the other three listened and injected an occasional expletive or one-liner. These were truly fun people to be with and the Jeep was alive with laughter and humorous tales.

Bernie is a language instructor at the University of Illinois in Champaign. Denny owns a coffee shop near campus. She had been a student of his at one time but had not done well in class as she was distracted by her immediate and overpowering attraction to the man. She made her affection known to him at her graduation and the two were soon dating, and eventually married.

I asked if there were any children and was told there were none.

Bernie said that neither of them "were equipped" – something they found out after they got married. Denny said that at first it put a strain on their relationship but they worked through it.

"Why ruin two families?" Bernie joked, half-heartedly. "Denny and I realized that if we two procreatively challenged individuals had married other people, there would now be two families incapable of having children."

"I think we'll adopt some day." Denny added. "What about you two, any plans?"

Jenna turned and looked at me, her face a mask of sadness. Tears threatened to flow but she choked them back and after an uncomfortable period of silence, that I'm sure our hosts felt as much as I did, she responded.

"I don't know," she whispered, and looked out the window at the passing countryside.

We drove on in silence for a while. Denny and I made sporadic small talk and Bernie silently drove the Jeep toward Colorado. Jenna stared out the window. I could almost hear the wheels spinning away as she puzzled through whatever it was that had so effectively captured her attention. Our hosts graciously allowed her silence.

We stopped for the night in Burlington, Colorado. Bernie and Denny got a room in a motel. Our cash was significantly depleted and I wanted to save as much as I could, so I asked Bernie if it would be all right if we slept in the Jeep. Denny offered to share their room with us and Bernie offered to pay for a room of our own, but I declined. I wanted some time alone to talk with Jenna, so sharing with our new friends was out. I was also uncomfortable having Bernie pay for a room when we would be perfectly comfortable in such a large vehicle. Jenna agreed with my feelings and thanked Bernie for the offer.

"Well then," Bernie said. "I guess we'll see you two in the morning! Breakfast is on me, no arguments!"

We agreed to that and parted company for the night. In the Jeep, I reached for Jenna's hand, and rather than pulling away, as I had expected, she clutched mine as if holding on for her life.

"What is wrong?" I insisted.

"I've just been thinking of how much I will miss. How much I won't be able to do."

I pulled her hand and drew her close so I could wrap my arms around her.

"Before I met you, Tory, I never thought about the things I would miss out on. Oh sure, I thought about making love, marriage, that sort of thing, but I never thought it would happen so I didn't dwell on it. Now you show up and all of that has changed. All of the things that normal couples have, I want. But, I can't have them."

"What things?" I asked. "We can still make love. We just have to take precautions."

"Children, Tory. Marriage. A home! A family! A life!"

Minstrel of a Modern Time

I sat silently, letting her vent her frustration on me. I knew I was the cause of these feelings she was having, just as much as she was the cause of the feelings that had suddenly surfaced in me.

"My God, Tory. I've found you. I've found the one man in the entire world that I could devote myself to. The one man to love like no other. The one who I could marry, settle down and have kids with. But it's all a big joke because I can't do those things. I'm dying. God knows that it might take years to run its course, but it's inevitable! I will die sooner or later, but most definitely sooner than I want to."

"Remember I asked you if you were afraid of death? I said that I was not afraid of death but afraid of dying. Remember that? At Woody's?"

"Yes," I replied.

"Well, I've been thinking about death since I met you and I realized that it's not death or dying that I'm afraid of. It's the possibility of *not* living or *not* enjoying my life to its fullest. Not finding all the answers to all the questions, or even worse, not even asking the questions. Not enjoying each sunrise for the unique miracle that it is. I want to live, Tory. I want to live with you. I want to find out just how far this love can carry us. But I can't! I can't!"

She broke down and cried uncontrollably for several minutes. I held her tightly, unsuccessfully fighting back my own tears. Finally her sobbing slowed and she looked out the window of the Jeep.

"I was stupid to think that I wouldn't feel this way eventually. I thought I could make it through to the end without letting depression overcome me. God, I'm only twenty-one. How could I think that I was so mature?"

"It's my fault," I said. "I should never have said anything about how I feel. We could have parted at the diner and that would have been that. Maybe I should leave."

Jenna stared at me as if I had two heads.

"You're a lot dumber than you look, McLeod."

I agreed.

"Then, maybe you should go home," I said. "I'll go with you."

She thought about this for some time.

"No," she said finally. "Our road leads west. That's where we'll go. But I should contact my parents. I haven't written to them in a while."

She retrieved a notepad and a pen from her rucksack.

"You might as well go to sleep," she said. "This will probably take a while."

I stretched out in the back of the Jeep facing the tailgate. I could hear her behind me, scribbling away. She cried softly as she wrote, sniffing periodically. Now and then she reached over the seat and stroked my hair. I wanted to stay awake – to wait until she was done, but sleep came anyway, followed by the dawn.

March 23 – Outside Lexington

Waylaid a bit in Lexington. No big thing, just a little trouble with locals. Back on track for Memphis now. Back on track with Bernie and Denny to follow.

After a fairly greasy, but delicious meal at a roadside diner, the four of us were back on the road. We passed through Denver and started the long climb into the mountains. It was a beautiful drive and before long we were in the vicinity of Vail.

Denny had directions on getting to her sister's house but either the directions weren't very good, Denny wasn't good at interpreting them, or Bernie wasn't good at following them, so we wandered the streets for over an hour before we found the house.

We were greeted at the front step by a large, growling Rottweiler. I had always had pretty good luck at befriending dogs, but thought it best that we wait until Denny's sister let the beast know that we were friends.

"Kaiser?" A voice called from inside the house. "Who's there?"

"Call off your boyfriend," Denny called from the driveway.

"Denny!"

A woman, who could have been Denny's twin,

although slightly older, threw open the screen door and rushed down the porch steps. Bernie, Jenna, Kaiser and I watched the reunion silently. I turned my attention to the enormous dog and patted my leg to call him over. He cocked his head slightly, as dogs often do when they are in doubt, and then walked cautiously over to me. I knelt down, and stroked the monster's side as he sniffed and then licked my face. Jenna watched me play with Kaiser and when I looked up at her she mouthed a single word.

Catalyst.

Denny provided the proper introductions, which to my surprise included Bernie. Apparently he and Kay had never met before, although they had spoken often on the telephone.

After everyone met everyone else, and Kaiser was satisfied that we were friendly, Kay asked if we were hungry and we all went inside for lunch. Kay invited us into the kitchen where we sat while she and Denny threw together soup and sandwiches for six. (Kaiser was included in every meal.)

While we ate, Jenna told our story, including the now routine lie about getting married in the Elvis Chapel. I began to think about the prospect of actually doing it when we got to Las Vegas. The more I thought about it, the better I liked the idea. I could imagine myself being married to her, coming home to meet you two, and settling down in Pennsylvania. I realized that it was something I really wanted to do. I knew I had to talk to her about it when we got some time alone.

The rest of the day and into the evening, the five of us explored Vail. Kay was the consummate guide, showing us all of the tourist sites before taking us to a nightclub for drinks and dancing. It's amazing to me to think that I had never danced a single time before I met Jenna at Barb O's, and there I was dancing my skinny butt off in a club in Vail, Colorado!

Fortunately for us, Kay maintained a sober mind as the four of us were fairly buzzed when we finally made the trip back to her house. Kaiser greeted us at the door but returned to his bed when he saw that we were all home safely. Kay broke out *Trivial Pursuit*, and challenged our intoxicated wits. We played until nearly 4:00am, laughing and joking about the questions. I don't remember if anyone actually won the game, but it didn't really matter.

Eventually we all said our "good nights" and wandered off to various corners of the house to sleep. Kay's house had three bedrooms, and Jenna and I shared one of the spares. I slept on the floor, as usual, and Jenna sprawled on the bed. We were both out cold within minutes of lying down.

I woke the next morning to the brilliant mountain sunshine, which triggered an explosion somewhere in my head. I have only been really drunk twice and both times was cursed with an excruciating hangover. I once met an EMT named Shawn who told me that the best thing for a hangover was oxygen. As I didn't have my own tank and mask, I decided to take a hike and suck in as much clean air as I could.

I stood and rubbed my eyes. A moan to my right revealed a waking, and equally hung over, Jenna. I sat on the bed next to her and stroked her hair.

"I'm going for a walk," I whispered.

"Stop shouting."

"You should go with me. The fresh air will clear your head."

Jenna opened a tentative eye and looked at me. I wanted her to go with me. It would give us an opportunity to talk.

"Please," I said.

Jenna responded by sitting up on her elbows and opening both eyes. The bright sunshine streaming through the window fell on her face causing her to grimace with pain. I put my arm around her waist and swung her around so her feet touched the floor.

"Come on," I said. "I want to talk to you about something."

I grabbed my sketching tools in case the Maestro decided to make an appearance. As we unlocked the front door, Kaiser lumbered up to join us. I didn't know if there was a leash law in the area but he seemed to be a well-behaved dog so I let him come along. The three of us walked down Kay's street, which ended in a cul-de-sac. Behind the houses at the end of the circle, the ground rose steadily. We walked up the hill along a well-beaten path until we came to a level area that overlooked the neighborhood. The view was stunning.

Near the center of the level area, a circle of stones outlined a dead, but recently used campfire. Sections of tree trunk surrounded the area, obviously used for stools. I sat down on one and drew in several lungfuls of the crisp air and felt my headache begin to wane. Kaiser sat down beside me and looked out over the valley.

A white wooden fence ran along the edge of a sharp drop-off on the north side of the level area. Jenna walked over to the fence and looked down. She stood there head down for a long time, and for a minute or so I thought that she might get sick. Instead, she glanced back over her shoulder and threw me a sly, but incredibly sexy smile. She then turned back toward the valley and let loose with possibly the worst yodeling I had ever heard.

"That's horrible," I said, and Kaiser twitched his ears in agreement.

"Come here," Jenna replied. "Join me. Let's wake up the neighborhood."

There was a time when I would have let such an invitation fall on deaf ears, but Jenna had a way of making ridiculous behavior seem fun. Kaiser and I walked over to the edge and stood there for a minute while Jenna proceeded to bellow into the valley. Kaiser joined her first, howling along with her terrible impersonation of Slim Whitman. Not wanting to be left out, I added my voice to the racket. The three of us stood on the edge of that ravine yodeling like maniacs, listening to the echo return from across the valley.

Eventually, the humor of the situation overcame me and I began to laugh. The combination of yodel and laugh conspired to give me a vicious case of hiccups, so I returned to the log stool to try to stop the spasms. Jenna and Kaiser remained at the edge, singing to the morning and most likely waking the dead as well as the neighborhood below.

When she had sufficiently fulfilled her wish, Jenna

came over and sat near me. Kaiser trotted over as well, sat next to Jenna and let her scratch behind his ears.

"Nice singing, Ringo," she said in a Liverpool accent as terrible as her yodeling.

"Another thing to check off your list," I said.

"Yep," she said with a cough. "Just think of what I would have missed if you hadn't been so damn loud this morning."

She laughed again and her laugh became a cough that lasted for several seconds. For the first time I really thought about her health. What would I do if she got sick while we were on the road? I didn't know how to take care of an AIDS patient! I didn't know what symptoms to expect or what kind of behavior to avoid or encourage. My knowledge of the affliction was limited at that point so I was not even aware of any treatment available to fight the effects of the disease.

"Are you all right?" I asked, reaching out for her hand.

"Yeah," she said through gasping breaths. "Thin air got to me. You're supposed to remind me to breathe."

"You're supposed to remind me to remind you," I replied.

A few more coughs and her breathing normalized.

"Better," she said. "What was it you wanted to talk about, my friend, my lover, my one-and-only Tory?"

Her smile stole the words from my mind that had been so clear the day before. I didn't know how to say what was spinning through my brain and was soon stammering like an idiot. I struggled for a few minutes, describing our relationship in obscure terms trying to relate my intentions by beating around as many bushes as I could manage. I think she figured out what I was driving at despite my inadequate dissertation. Finally I gave up and spit it out.

"In short, will you marry me? I mean for real."

She sat for a minute holding as perfect a poker face as I have ever seen, then began laughing.

"Well, that wasn't so hard after all, was it?"

"I'm serious," I said.

"Why?"

"Why? Why what? Why am I serious, or why do I want to marry you?"

"Yeah."

What a question! Why? It was one of the few responses I didn't expect. I expected her to say *yes*, even *no*, but *why*? It still baffles me.

I told her that I felt it would validate our relationship. It would complete something in both of us. It would make us one. I told her that it was the natural next step in a love so deep and true. I told her a dozen other things, all as pathetically romantic and philosophical as the others, and she just sat there listening with that twisted sarcastic grin on her face. I was eventually so flustered that I threw up my arms in defeat.

"Because I want to!" I shouted, hoping to punctuate all of the other reasons that seemed to fall flat.

Jenna shook her head and snickered. I was sure she was going to say that it was the most ridiculous idea she had ever heard.

"Good enough reason for me, I guess. You're on McLeod."

I gaped at her. She had accepted! She had put me through ten minutes of stuttering gibberish just to play with me!

"You are so aggravating!" I shouted. "I sit here pouring out reason after reason why we should get married and you settle for *because I want to*! I think I'll just take it back! I've changed my mind!"

"Too late," she said, and tackled me to the ground, covering my face with kisses. Kaiser watched us rolling around on the dewy ground and decided it was his kind of fun and soon we were wrestling with a 110-pound dog as well.

Jenna began coughing again and pulled herself from the pile. She stood up and walked back toward the fence with her hands on her hips, hacking away like a life-long smoker. I rose and walked toward her but she waved me off before I got close enough to touch her.

"I'm ok," she said, taking several deep breaths.

"No you're not," I said. "We should go back inside."

"Not yet," she wheezed. "I'm ok, really. Listen, you brought your sketchpad. Why don't you make yourself useful and draw something for our hostess?"

I walked closer and asked if she was truly all right. She hugged me tightly, telling me that she was better than all right, that she was truly happy, and that for the first time since she was diagnosed with the virus, she was excited about the future. I fell into her, feeling our souls blend into one. I whispered my love into her ear and felt her embrace tighten. We stood there for several minutes hugging each other, feeling emotions sweep over us until a very canine groan brought us out of our reverie. Kaiser sat nearby watching the two of us, apparently feeling very left out.

"I think that we should get a dog," Jenna whispered. "But not one so dumb, or so ugly."

He responded to Jenna's tease with a short bark.

"Oh, I didn't mean you, handsome. You are beautiful and intelligent. I think the blank look and constant drooling add to your abundant charm."

She grabbed the big dog around the neck and held his hairy face between her hands.

"You are truly the Don Juan of your breed."

I watched the two of them and the Maestro tickled the surface. I returned to the stump and opened the sketchpad. The blank page in front of me was soon covered with lines, forming an image of the scene in front of me. Jenna and Kaiser, nose to nose, smiles on their respective faces and affection in their eyes.

When I finished, I told Jenna to stand back at the fence and look back at me like she had before. The Maestro started a new picture, this one of my beautiful bride-to-be, looking back over her shoulder, her long blonde hair flowing like a mane and that ever-so sexy pencil-thin smile. You'll find the results of that drawing session included in this package. It was not the only drawing I made of her, but I think it was one of the best. I really hope you like it. We returned to Kay's house to find Bernie sitting at the kitchen table, nursing a cup of coffee.

"Good morning fellow travelers," he said over the rim of his mug. "Our kind hostess has sped off to the supermarket for breakfast materials. I have managed to brew up some truly tasteless coffee if you're feeling the need for a boost."

Jenna poured us both a mug and we joined Bernie at the table. He noticed the sketchpad and asked if he could see what I had been working on. I showed him the two drawings I had just completed and he seemed very impressed. I told him that the one of Jenna and Kaiser was for Kay, which he declared *a fine gift*. He then asked if he could commission me to do a drawing of Denny. I told him that I had already planned one of the both of them but that he had already paid me by sharing a ride and his company.

"Well then," he said. "I would like you to also do one of yourself and your lovely fiancée. I should like to have something to remember you by when we finally part company and your skillful hand could do you better justice than any photograph."

I was flattered. I think Jenna was as well. I had never done a drawing of myself and if fact I doubted I could actually draw myself from memory. Nevertheless, I agreed.

Jenna told Bernie about the drawing I had done of Harlan and Dorlene in Harlan's Impala. The mention of the car reminded me of the "totem" concept I had stumbled upon while washing it. I had not mentioned this concept to Jenna yet, and took that opportunity to bring it up for her and Bernie. Bernie was intrigued by the idea and wondered at what I thought the "totem" was that symbolized Denny and himself. I told him I didn't know but I'd look for it.

"Denise!" He called loudly down the hallway to the

first floor guest room. "Rise and shine, lovey! We're all starving here waiting for you to make us some breakfast."

"Eat shit," came the response from the room. "Pardon my French."

"Actually, my dear. The French would say *Merde mangez*." He replied with a smile.

"Yeah, well, good for the French," Denny moaned.

Bernie topped off his coffee and returned to the table.

"She wasn't much of a student when I had her in class. But, she took a fancy to the vulgarities of the languages she studied. Now my sweet little Denny can curse like a sailor in at least five languages."

We all laughed until we noticed that Denny had joined us in the kitchen. Her squinted eyes and furrowed brow betrayed her hangover. We all fell silent and then, as if on cue, broke into laughter again.

"You people are sick," Denny said as she found a mug and poured herself some coffee.

Kay returned with two bags of groceries and set them on the counter.

"Well, there's enough eggs and bacon in there to feed us all including Kaiser," she said and we all cheered.

"You people are so loud," Denny said from behind her hands, which supported her aching head. "Sick and loud."

We spent the entire day at Kay's. Jenna watered the flower gardens that surrounded the house and I found a bucket and some soap and washed and waxed her car and Bernie's Jeep. Bernie, Denny, and Kay went into town for a few hours and left Jenna and I to mind the house and keep Kaiser out of mischief. I was touched by Kay's almost innate trust in us to leave her house and dog in our care. We made sure to justify that trust.

The three of us lounged in Kay's fenced-in backyard under a good-sized oak tree. Kaiser was soon sleeping heavily in the sun while Jenna and I cuddled in a lounge chair. We made love again, this time taking precautions by using a condom that Jenna had purchased from a machine in the ladies room of the nightclub we visited. It was a fairly warm day and the heat combined with the thin air soon put us both to sleep. Fortunately we had the forethought to dress before we fell asleep, as Bernie and company returned while we were still in dreamland.

Kay had bought a do-it-yourself framing kit to mount the drawing of Jenna and Kaiser. She was genuinely touched by the picture and wanted to hang it in the living room for all who visited her to see. Denny gave Jenna and me matching Denver Broncos sweatshirts and new sneakers to replace our old, road-worn pairs. She had apparently gotten our shirt and shoe sizes in the middle of the night while we were comatose. We thanked her profusely, both of us feeling humbled by her generosity.

Bernie took me aside and gave me gifts of his own. A new sketchpad, with a spiral spine to allow the pages to easily turn back without folding, and two new boxes of artist's pencils – one set in 32 colors.

"I noticed that your pencils had worn down to nubs," he said.

I felt choked with emotion. These gifts, and the shirt and shoes that Denny had given me, were not given out of pity or compassion. These were not gifts of food or money or shelter. They were gifts of friendship. Not since my parents were alive had I been given something so special. I felt my hands shaking as I held the metal pencil boxes.

Jenna approached and slipped her arm around my waist. I felt her cheek lean against my shoulder but I couldn't take my eyes off the pencils. I wanted to thank Bernie and Denny but couldn't find the right words. Simply saying "thank you" could not convey the emotions I felt. I looked to Jenna who stepped in and found the words for me.

"Bernard Morissette, you are a genuine angel. Your generosity is as priceless as your gift."

She leaned up and kissed him on the cheek. He blushed and tried to fend off the compliment with a bit of wit. Jenna then gave Denny and Kay each a big hug and thanked them for their kindness and friendship.

I stood next to Bernie, clutching the sketchpad and pencil boxes as if they might fly away if I loosened my grip. I was completely flustered. Finally, a few words found their way to my lips.

"I've never worked with colors before."

"Well," Bernie said, returning to his normal jovial self, "I suppose you'd better get cracking then! You've got work to do laddie, make haste!"

I walked toward the house, intending to begin the portrait I promised. As I approached the back door, I turned and found the words I had been searching for. Ironically, they were the very words I previously felt were so inadequate.

"Thank you, Denny. Thank you Bernie."

"You're welcome," Bernie said softly. "Now draw boy! Draw!"

I found it difficult at first to use the colors and produce as accurate a rendering as I could with the plain black pencils. When you draw with black only you draw the shadows of things. But when you draw with color you draw the light. I had never tried to draw the light before and it took several sheets off my old sketchpad before I was able to produce the highlights and flesh tones that would make for a decent portrait.

I sketched my hand, an old warm-up technique that I used when I had not sketched in some time. I sketched some of the objects in Kay's kitchen, to get used to capturing light rather than shadow. I sketched Kaiser a number of times, trying to bring out the life in his eyes. I must have practiced for two or three hours before I finally set to the portrait I had promised. But the Maestro was not comfortable with these new tools. I could not seem to capture the shape of Bernie's face or the slant of Denny's eyes. I finally decided to do the portrait in black and white first, and then try to reproduce it in color.

But what does this have to do with Jenna? Nothing, so I'll stop rambling on about it and simply say that the portrait was finally completed. Bernie and Denny loved it. I was not overly thrilled with the outcome. Jenna assured me that I had successfully captured our two friends. I felt that the skin was a little too yellow and I couldn't exactly match the redness of Denny's hair. Jenna told me that nobody likes a perfectionist. Kay asked if she could keep the black and white portraits and I gave them to her.

All in all it wasn't a failed attempt. But I was determined to do a better job on the portrait of Jenna and myself that I had also promised. I somehow managed to do it. When it was done, Jenna added her scribbled signature below mine. She then wrote a rather lengthy message on the backside of the drawing, thanking them again for their kindness and friendship, and wishing them the best for their future.

I insisted on buying dinner that night, although my severely depleted funds could only afford pizza and beer. We stayed in that night. Denny and Kay reminisced about their childhood, growing up in Oceanside, New York. Bernie talked about growing up in Brighton, England, and his emigration to America in the early 80's. Jenna, Kaiser and I sat and listened.

As the night progressed Denny asked me to play something on my guitar. Jenna insisted that I tell them about Erik. They all found the story to be amusing, and asked to see where I had scratched the name in the guitar's neck. When that was out of the way, I began with a few of my upbeat songs, and then took requests. Bernie tried to stump me by requesting Mozart's *Eine Kleine Nacht Musik*, but I managed to pick out a fair interpretation.

At some point during the concert Kay left the room and returned with her own guitar. She said that her guitar did not have a name but she had been playing for several years and wondered if I would be interested in a duet. We proceeded to harmonize our way through a number of Beatles, Eagles and Dylan tunes. Jenna joined in on a few songs, and despite her pathetic yodeling earlier that morning she managed to carry the tune and added her own harmony.

We sang and played and drank until 2:00am when Bernie said that he needed to get some sleep in order to be awake enough to continue our trip to Las Vegas. Denny followed shortly after and Jenna was soon asleep on the living room couch. Kay and I stayed up for a bit talking about a variety of things. She told me that she envied my courage to live the way I did. She said that there had been times during college when she had considered the same sort of lifestyle but her parents had high hopes for her and she didn't want to disappoint them so she stayed on and completed her degree in psychology.

We talked until nearly 3:30 before she finally decided to go to bed. She thanked me for playing and singing with her and gave me a kiss on the cheek before disappearing into her room. I curled up on the floor next to Kaiser and quickly fell asleep. It had been another eventful, exhausting day.

We left Kay's around noon. We said our good-bye's by the Jeep, with plenty of hugs and kisses, and licks where Kaiser was concerned. Kay told Jenna and me that we were welcome to stop by any time we were in the area. Denny and Bernie both promised Kay that they would visit more often and Kay promised the same to them. Then after a half hour of last words we were off.

The trip through the mountains was incredible, although Jenna and I both wished we were on foot as we were not able to enjoy it quite as much from a speeding car. We didn't rush the trip.

We stopped occasionally to enjoy the scenery, and to yodel a bit, although Jenna seemed to get worse at it as time went on. Kay had packed us with enough groceries to last a few days, and there were enough hotels and motels scattered along the way that we spent our one night on the road indoors, which is a shame as the skies were clear and full of stars that night.

I practiced with my new colored pencils nearly all the way, eventually learning the right combinations of colors necessary to produce a variety of skin tones. Several pages of my old sketchpad were covered with small drawings of trees, road signs, and several dozen miscellaneous sketches of my traveling companions.

Jenna rewrote her wish list to include only the things that she really wanted to accomplish. Having completed three of her wishes already, she wanted to take a serious stab at completing as many of the others as she could. Next to each item was a space for a date, and a short comment on the experience. She filled in the dates of the three items she had already managed to complete.

Passing through Utah we had a very strange experience. We passed a lone hitchhiker thumbing his way toward some unknown destination. I was struck with a strange sense of disorientation, as if I was seeing myself out there on the road. A shudder ran through me and I thought: *That's me out there. That's what I look like. That's what all we road nomads look like.*

I told Jenna what I was feeling and she said that she had the same feelings as we drove past the man. It was spooky. I knew what was going through that man's mind. I felt the emptiness in his stomach, the heat of the sun on his back, the throb of his feet where the tightness of his boots had worn blisters on his tendons and toes. But mostly I felt his frustration as another car, this one containing a mirror image of him, drove by without slowing down.

I asked Bernie to stop and pick the man up. We were already a few miles past him, but I felt such an incredible imbalance in my soul at the thought of passing him by. I explained my feelings to Bernie who seemed to understand. Denny commented that she felt something strange, like déjà vu, when we passed him as well. We had room for one more on the bench seat in the back, and with only a minor bit of coaxing, Bernie turned the Jeep around and drove back toward the man.

We backtracked for two or three miles, but the man was nowhere to be seen. The landscape was wide open on both sides of the highway, so there was no place for him to hide. He was simply not there. Everyone in the car silently scanned the countryside for any sign of the man or his gear. There was nothing to be seen but the wide-open plains of the desert, and the mountains in the distance. Without a word, Bernie turned the Jeep back and we resumed our trip in silence. I was never one to believe in ghosts, but to this day I wonder about that man. If it was a hallucination, why did we all have it? If it was a mirage, why was it so detailed?

I broke out my drawing tools and tried to capture what I had seen. When I finished I showed it to Jenna. She agreed with everything I had drawn except she insisted that the man was wearing a wide brimmed hat, like the kind Clint Eastwood wore in his Westerns. I hadn't noticed a hat. Denny said the man wasn't wearing a hat, but was wearing sunglasses. But I distinctly recall seeing his eyes. Bernie said that the man had long hair tied in a ponytail, but I remember it being short, like a military cut. We had all seen the same thing, but had seen it differently.

I have no idea what significance or lesson we were supposed to draw from that sighting. As I think back on it, perhaps the phantom was a representative of all who travel the roads. Perhaps, he was a reflection of myself, or Jenna, or Bernie, or Denny for that matter – perhaps all of us. Maybe that's why we all saw something different.

Still, thinking back, I get that same sense of disorientation, as if my eyes had seen myself during some strange out of body episode.

The silence of that little trip into the Twilight Zone stayed with us for several miles. It was finally broken by Bernie announcing our arrival in Nevada.

"Only a few more miles and we'll be in the city of Lost Wages," he declared. "Are you a gambling man, Tory?"

"No," I replied. "I've never had enough scratch to feel comfortable about throwing it away."

"Well, then, I'd like to front you a few bucks and see how you do. I get a feeling you may be fairly good at beating the odds."

I argued with him about it for while. I told him that to a person like me, treating money with such disrespect was as unthinkable as throwing a Bible in the trash would be to a Born Again Christian.

"Then stand with me a while and help me win. I'll give you half of whatever I win. Fair enough?"

Bernie was not the type of man who understood the word "no." He would continue to change the arrangement until I finally gave in. I was in no mind to carry out a debate for that long so I agreed to *assist* him at the tables. Jenna was no help, either. She took Bernie's side and tried to convince me that this would be fun.

"What have *you* got to lose?" She asked.

I was suddenly very nervous as the only real gambling I had ever witnessed was in the back alley of a men's hotel in St. Louis. I had not participated myself, simply watched from the side. I was able to understand the rules of the game and decided it was time to move on when I realized that the man taking bets was cheating. There was sure to be a fight, and possibly a murder, and I wanted to be as far away as possible when the losers finally checked the dice. Now I was on my way to the gambling capital of the Solar System and had agreed to help Bernie lose his money.

The desert sky was darkening through the colors of the spectrum as the sun dipped below the horizon. I always loved nighttime in the desert. The air is clean. The sky is devoid of clouds. Stars, many of which can only be seen in such a dark, isolated place, shine down with light that left them millions of years ago. And silence, unmatched by anything except the tomb, settles in with the darkness. I love the desert.

Jenna curled up next to me and looked out my window. She asked about several stars that began poking through the fabric of the sky. It was difficult to identify many of them without some sort of reference, but I took a stab, which turned out to be right as often as it was wrong. Denny joined in and our astronomy lesson lasted until the glow of Las Vegas began to pollute the sky.

Going to stop now. I see a few trucks coming my way and I'm betting I can get a bit further down the road today. With any luck, one of them is going to Memphis!

March 24 – Memphis, TN

Made it! Haven't been over to Graceland yet but I plan on spending a few days here so I'll get around to it. I still have some cash from Cincy so I'm staying at the YMCA while I'm here. Hot showers! Gotta love 'em!

Now, I had been to Las Vegas before, passing through on my way west. I had only stayed one night and managed to earn enough to get a bus ticket to Bakersfield and a meal. The meal, mind you, was at one of the many buffets Las Vegas is noted for, and I managed to pack away several plates of a variety of foods for a mere seven bucks. But I didn't gamble while I was there. I didn't even take the time to watch other gamble. I wasn't interested.

Bernie pulled up in front of the Frontier Hotel and Casino. We unloaded our gear and made our way to the front desk. I knew that he was going to offer us a room, and I couldn't think of a way to politely decline. We couldn't possibly sleep in the Jeep, parked in some hotel back lot. Besides, ever since the coughing spell on the hill in Vail, I had been watching Jenna with a concerned eye. The coughing had not repeated but I was worried that she might become ill if she didn't have a warm bed, and even warmer food. My pride had to take a back seat to my concern for her health so when Denny walked over and dropped a room key in my lap I thanked her and accepted it.

"First things first," Bernie said, rubbing his palms rapidly together. "Buffet!"

I couldn't argue with that! Neither could Jenna. We followed our two friends up to our room, which was across the hallway from their own, and stowed our gear. Then we all descended on the hotel's buffet like a pack of rabid dogs. We must have eaten for a good two hours, Bernie and Denny keeping pace with Jenna and me. A small food fight broke out at our table, and our clothes were soon spotted with tomato sauce, gravy and mashed potatoes.

When the meal was over, we went back to the room to change out of our stained clothes. I thought about staying in the room hoping Bernie would head to the casino without me, but a knock on the door quickly changed that tune. Jenna answered it. Bernie stepped in wearing a black suit and tapped out a cigarette from a metal case.

"Bond," he said, as he lit up. "James Bond."

Jenna giggled.

"Denise would like to have a word with you Mademoiselle," Bernie said, holding the door so Jenna could slip across the hall.

I tried to plead with Bernie to leave me behind. I didn't mind if Jenna wanted to go off and play in the casino, but I was content to stay in and watch something on TV.

"Nonsense, Mr. McLeod. The night is young.

We've reached our destination. Come boy, you need a suit!"

He grabbed my arm and led me out into the hallway. Denny stayed behind waiting for Jenna who was taking an inordinate amount of time in the bathroom. Despite my tickling concern, I allowed Bernie to lead me to the elevator.

We went into a men's clothing store down one of the side corridors of the hotel. After trying on several suits of different cuts, but all black per his instructions, we settled on a double-breasted suit and black linen band-collar shirt. With the proper shoes and some blood red socks, the whole outfit looked very sharp, even on me. Still, my hair was a mess, looking something like a lion's mane with a few birds nest trapped in it.

"Now, for a bit of sprucing up," Bernie said as he tossed a credit card to the shopkeeper.

Down the hall from the men's shop was a barber. Bernie dragged me in and spun me into the seat. About an hour later, the stubble was shaved from my face, my hair was clean, combed, trimmed up and tied back in a neat ponytail, and my fingernails were neatly manicured. I looked in the mirror and didn't recognize the face looking back at me. I had never seen that person before. I began to feel those same emotions well up in me that arose when Bernie gave me the art kit.

Bernie walked up behind me and looked into the mirror with a broad, satisfied smile on his face.

"Excuse me, sir. I'm looking for a friend of mine. Oh Tory! It's you. Good show. You clean up nicely. Come now. Flowers for the ladies!"

We picked out corsages for Denny and Jenna. By this point I was just going with the flow and actually enjoying this little fairy tale makeover. Bernie put a red carnation in my lapel. He put a white one with green tinted fringe in his own jacket. We then returned to the room to get the ladies.

As we walked I asked Bernie why he had done all this. He told me that he and Denny felt strangely attracted to the two of us, as if we were younger versions of them.

"We've rather enjoyed your company," he said. "And we've grown very fond of both of you. I have a feeling our paths will part soon, and we wanted to give you a little pre-wedding present of sorts."

I told him that I would like to somehow pay him for the suit. He told me to help him win at the tables and that would be payment enough. Added pressure to my already twitching nerves!

As we rounded a corner in the hallway that led to the room, we both stopped dead in our tracks. Denny and Jenna were coming down the hall. Had I not recognized that thin, sexy smile, I would not have known that it was Jenna.

"Oh my," Bernie said.

The two were breathtaking. Denny's long red hair hung loosely over her shoulders. An ample application of hair products made those fiery tresses stand around her face like a flaming aura. She wore a mid-thigh emerald green evening dress and matching shoes. Jenna was in an equivalent length, blood red dress and shoes. Her hair was pulled back tightly from her face and bound in a ponytail with a spiraling red ribbon. Both women carried the knowledge of their beauty with each graceful step.

Denny strolled up to Bernie and gave him a peck on the cheek, leaving a slight smudge of lipstick. Jenna similarly approached me.

"Breathe," she whispered in my ear, following the kiss.

"Wrong green," Denny said, pressing her nose up to Bernie's carnation. "But, close enough."

I realized she was referring to the tint of the carnation and the color of her dress. Bernie had picked the flowers based on what our partners were wearing. The whole thing had been planned right down to the finest detail.

Denny turned toward me and ran her long fingers up and down the lapel of my suit. I'm sure I blushed profusely, but definitely enjoyed the attention.

"Nice," she said. "You did well with this one Bernard."

"Yes," Bernie said with a grin, and seemed to drift for a moment. "But, lo! The night awaits! There are drinks to be drunk and chips to be won!"

With that, the ladies stepped in front to lead the way. It wasn't until the moment when they passed in front of us, that either of us realized that the dresses were cut extremely low in the back. We both gasped audibly and then followed our ladies with our mouths hanging agape.

That night we visited Caesar's Palace, The Mirage, The Flamingo, and two or three other casinos. Everywhere we went we turned heads – well, our ladies did anyway. Denny and Jenna spent a lot of time at the roulette table, and managed to break even. Bernie was a better gambler than he let on, particularly at card games. He and I sat at several different blackjack tables and did respectably well, but nothing to write home about.

I played very conservatively, particularly because it wasn't my money I was wasting. Bernie encouraged me to be a bit more aggressive, especially at blackjack where I seemed to win more often than I lost. And, I must admit I did have a lot of fun despite my uneasiness at risking something that I rarely had – money.

We attacked each casino with a game plan – divide and conquer, then meet at the bar in an hour. If one of us did well, we would stay another hour. If the games were cold, we would move on. The bigger casinos were all cold. For the most part we broke even or made a little – nothing spectacular. It wasn't until we found ourselves at 3:00am in some unremarkable club in the downtown district that we really started to hit it big.

I sat in on a $5 blackjack game and proceeded to do fairly well. Bernie fronted me $200 and then disappeared into another room. I managed to double my money, making sure to pocket my winnings so as not to lose more than I sat down with. When the first hour was up, I made my way to the bar to meet with my colleagues and discuss the game plan.

Jenna and Denny moved from roulette to craps and managed to nail their bets time after time. As they were easily the most beautiful women in the place, they were quickly elected to throw the dice by the businessmen and locals playing along side them. They stood at the end of the table, arms around each other's waist, Jenna placing the bets and Denny "rolling the bones." They managed to win over $1500 before meeting me at the door.

Bernie was nowhere to be seen. We waited for nearly 20 minutes before Denny asked me to look for him. I walked back to the room where he had vanished and found him sitting at a poker table with four other men and two women. Bernie signaled for me to come and stand behind him. The others at the table looked at me suspiciously.

The dealer asked me if I intended to join the game. If not, I was to sit away from the table.

"He will join the game," Bernie said. "He'll be taking my place."

I tried to object, but Bernie rose and pulled me to the chair. The dealer asked if there were any objections in the switch. Apparently Bernie had been taking his toll on his opponents so none of them were sorry to see him go. I pulled Bernie close and whispered in his ear.

"I don't know how to play this game."

"Nobody really does," he whispered back.

I looked at Bernie's pile of chips. There was easily $5000 in front of me. That's more money than I had seen pass through my hands in the last two years combined! I began to get very nervous which I'm sure showed and made the other players all the more confident in their decision to let me play. Then the dealer threw the cards.

I knew the basics of poker – the various hands, which ones are better than other, that sort of thing. But I had no idea how to bet. Bernie had put me in charge of a large stack of chips and I started right in losing them.

"Let the Maestro play," Bernie said from across the room.

I had never thought of the Maestro as a gambler, but he was the one with the hidden abilities. If anyone could make a fair stand at this game, he would be better suited than me. All I had to do was draw him out – literally.

Before me was a small pad of paper, presumably for passing notes to the dealer or waiters when they came by. I picked up the pencil next to the pad and let the Maestro come to the surface. I called him out by sketching the face of the woman across from me. When he had surfaced, I put the pencil down and looked at the cards with his eyes.

I played for nearly two hours. At some point, Bernie had retrieved Jenna and Denny and the three of them sat at the bar on the far side of the room we were in. After several hands I got the hang of betting – when to call, when to fold, when to raise. I paid no attention to the chips in front of me, only to the cards and the other people at the table. I eventually picked up a few hints of what Bernie referred to as the players' "tells" which helped me determine if they were bluffing or had a good hand.

Two of the other players dropped out of the game somewhere along the way. Periodically I felt the Maestro slip away and picked up the pencil and drew someone else at the table. Bernie brought me drinks, mostly ice water, and offered some vague praise to my play, which I barely heard.

The game was intense. I had never seen that much money in cash, chips, or any other kind of representation.

I played like a man possessed. Time flew by with each hand until my friends at the bar decided that enough was enough.

"Mr. McLeod," I heard Bernie call from across the room. "I think it's time we left. These two lovelies are getting a bit hungry."

"In a minute," I said, never taking my eyes off the cards.

"Tory," he said more firmly. "Let it go."

I looked at Bernie across the room. I had been completely oblivious to the three of them for the past hour. Jenna sat on a stool with her head lying on the bar. She looked exhausted. Denny and Bernie were sitting at a nearby table, Denny's head resting in Bernie's lap. Bernie sat slouched, a lit cigarette smoldering between his fingers. They all looked like they'd had enough for one night. Part of me, the Maestro, wanted to tell them to go on without me. I was hot. The game was intense, and I thought I could keep the streak going until all the other players left. But, as the Maestro slipped away, my better judgment returned and I told them we would leave after the current hand.

I lost that hand. But true to my word I picked up my winnings and left the game. Before actually leaving the room, I signed each of the sketches and gave them to the respective players. Only one of them – one of the ladies – thanked me for it.

In the end I had pushed Bernie's stack to around $8000. He had entered the game with $3000 so that meant between us we had won over $5000! Altogether, between Denny and Jenna at the craps table, me at the blackjack table, and Bernie and me at the poker game, we won just under $7,000!

We cashed in the chips and called a limo. Bernie said that when you win that much money it's best to stay in the casino until your ride appears, especially in the part of town we were in. When the car pulled up we slipped in and hit the early morning streets.

We pigged out at another buffet, eating mostly breakfast foods, but sneaking in a piece of pizza or fried chicken as well. At one point during the meal Denny and Jenna left for the restroom. Bernie took advantage of their absence to give me what he said was my share of the winnings. He tried to give me over half but I argued with him that his deal had been for half and not a penny more. He laughed and split the money down the middle. I then took my stack and peeled off enough to pay for the suit and shoes, the hair cut, the room and Jenna's dress. He tried to refuse but I insisted. I even insisted on paying for the meal!

With our stomachs and pockets full we called it a night and sometime around 9:00am, we returned to our rooms. Jenna and I curled up on the bed, nestled like spoons, still wearing our evening clothes. It was the first time in over a year that I had actually slept in a bed, but I was too exhausted to feel uncomfortable and within minutes we were both out cold.

March 25 – Still in Memphis

I'm excited to start this next part so I took a break to gather my thoughts and clear my head with some good sleep time. The next part of our story represents the greatest joy I've ever experienced and starts to explain how things began to unravel. I hope I do it justice.

I didn't sleep for very long, perhaps two or three hours. I find it difficult to sleep during the day and noontime was rolling around. I opened the curtains a bit and looked out into the day. The sun was brilliant and heat waves rose from the pavement. It was a good day to get married.

I took a quick shower, letting the steam remove some of the wrinkles from my suit before putting it back on. I opened the dresser drawer and found a thick telephone book. I fumbled through the Yellow Pages until I found what I was looking for – the Elvis Chapel. I called the number listed and asked what was required to get married there. The man on the other end of the line, who spoke with a pitiful Elvis voice, informed me that all of the paperwork could be taken care of on site and that all I had to do is bring myself and my "little hunka-hunka burnin' love" on down.

Jenna was still asleep when I went down to the florist

shop off the hotel's main casino. I bought her two-dozen red roses and a box of rose petals. I then ordered lunch for the four of us to be delivered to our room. I also stopped at a gift shop and found two matching silver and turquoise rings. As I walked by the casino, I saw the blank stares of the regulars who blindly plunked their money into slot machines. I silently thanked Bernie for yanking me away from the poker game before the fever really got a hold on me.

I spread the rose petals all around the room and scattered half of the roses on the bed where Jenna lay dead to the world. Now that I've written that, I wish I had used a pencil so I could erase it. What an awful thing to say. I'm so sorry.

Anyway, Jenna didn't wake up until the food arrived. I had all of it set up in our room and then went and pounded on the door to Bernie's room. A very groggy Denny answered the door. I told her that lunch was served in our room and that I had a surprise planned for everyone. She agreed to wake Bernie and join us. Jenna, meanwhile, was lying on the bed sniffing at the rose buds near her head.

"I love these," she said as I returned to the room. "It's too bad they don't last forever, but then nothing beautiful really does."

I couldn't tell if she was talking about herself or our relationship, but I knew that there was a double meaning in her comment.

"Bernie and Denny are coming over for lunch," I said. "After we eat, I have a surprise for you."

"Another surprise, McLeod?" She said slowly rising

from the rose strewn bed. "People will begin to talk."

"I hope so."

"Did I tell you how good you look in that suit?"

"Yes."

"You should get it cleaned while we're here."

"Later," I said. I wanted to wear the suit to the chapel. I thought it would be nice to get married in our evening clothes, rather than in the wrinkled jeans and T-shirts stuffed in our packs. But she didn't know what I had in mind so I changed the subject and talked about the night before.

Bernie and Denny showed up and we all ate the feast before us. Afterward, I told the three of them to get cleaned up while I went and made some arrangements for the surprise I had planned. I went to the lobby and used the desk phone to call a limo.

I can't describe the feeling I had spending money so frivolously. I had never had more than $50 at a time, not counting the wad that Harlan and Dorlene slipped me, so finding myself with over $2000 in hand gave me a kind of vague need to spend it recklessly. Bernie's aggressive lust for life must have been contagious.

The limo arrived shortly before Jenna and company met me in the lobby. I told the driver where we were going, but asked him to keep it quiet, as my companions had no idea what I was up to. When the three of them finally came down from the room, I herded them into the limo and we were off.

Even though I was completely committed to Jenna, and regardless of the silly location of the ceremony, I had butterflies just thinking about the prospect of being married. My hands shook. I broke out in a cold sweat. I was nervous but joyful.

The cat was out of the bag the moment we pulled up in front of the chapel. Jenna's mouth fell open and Bernie cheered. I paid the driver and we scrambled out of the limo and into the chapel.

We were seventh in line to get married that afternoon so we sat and waited through the other ceremonies, each as silly and campy as the next. With only two more to go before our turn, Jenna got up and disappeared into a back room. I wondered if she had second thoughts. Denny got up and followed her.

While we sat, I asked Bernie if he would be the Best Man. He said that he might not be the "best" man but he would certainly give it his best attempt. I handed him the rings telling him that I was somewhat embarrassed that they were not the traditional gold bands. He reassured me telling me that they were perfect, considering all of the circumstances.

"Besides," he said, "it's not the metal of the ring counts, but rather the mettle of the man. The ring is a symbol. It's your courage to commit yourself that is the true mark."

The sixth wedding was nearly over and Jenna was still nowhere to be seen. I began wondering if I had been left at the altar, but when the "reverend" in the black leather jacket called us forward, she appeared at the back of the chapel. I turned to watch her walk down the aisle and was presented with a bride like no other the world has ever seen.

She came down the aisle carrying a bouquet of fake

daises with Denny by her side. Bernie and I gaped and then broke into gales of laughter as we saw Jenna dressed as the King himself strolling down the aisle!

She wore a white faux leather jumpsuit, complete with cape and high collar, decorated with studs and rhinestones and flared at the bottom to accommodate the matching white leather boots. On her fingers she wore a half-dozen ultra-gaudy rings, which caught the light in their fake stones as she posed and shook her hands at us. But the best part of the whole outfit was on her head. She wore the characteristic Elvis sunglasses, an enormous black wig complete with mutton chop sideburns, and a sneer that only Elvis himself could have bettered!

I was literally floored. I fell to my knees holding my sides, tears streaming from my eyes. Bernie was laughing so hard he was hardly breathing. Even the Elvis-impersonator officiating the ceremony was cracking up. In fact, the only two people in the entire chapel who *weren't* laughing were Denny and Jenna – I mean Elvis. She walked up to the podium, gave a karate kick, and dropped into a pose.

"Thank ye verah much," she said, pointing one of her ringed fingers at Bernie and me.

I continued laughing feeling like I was going to wet my pants. Bernie somehow got to his feet and dragged me up with him.

"If you're not going to take this seriously we'll take our business elsewhere," Denny said with a poker face that would shame even the Maestro.

"That's right," Jenna sneered. "Don't be cruel little

mama, or you'll be spendin' the night at the Heartbreak Hotel."

The Elvis-in-charge opened his book and began the ceremony. The whole event was ludicrous – the vows, the verbiage, even the musical interlude of *Love Me Tender*. But as ridiculous at it was, when the papers were signed it was legal. At 4:45pm on June 10th, Jenna and I became man and wife.

Even now as I write about that moment I find myself giggling, and my free hand makes its way to the chain around my neck that hold both of our wedding rings. I wish you two could have been there. I wish my folks could have been there too. It was some kind of event, that's for sure.

We spent the rest of that day bombing around Vegas in the limo. We rented the Elvis suit from the chapel and Jenna made several "appearances" at convenience stores and doughnut shops throughout the city. I wonder how much of that showed up in the tabloids that year! *Elvis spotted at his favorite gas station in Las Vegas!*

We finally returned the suit and limo around dinnertime and made our way back to the Frontier to eat. After dinner, Denny and Jenna each took a cupful of quarters and played the slot machines while Bernie and I watched a baseball game on the TV in the bar. We toasted the day and as Bernie put it, "the most bizarre nuptials" he had ever attended.

Jenna and I hit the bed early that night. Enough said.

I had a dream that night that I was in a forest of enormous trees. I was alone and standing on a wooden footbridge. I felt a great despair and loss. I called out again and again.

"Jenna! Jenna!"

As I tried to cross the small bridge, it seemed to stretch and narrow until it was a swaying bridge of ropes and planks, suspended over a gorge a thousand feet deep. I called out for Jenna to help me, telling her I couldn't survive without her, but my pleas were lost against the wind. I tried to balance myself and move slowly, eventually getting down on my hands and knees to crawl across the bridge, but the wind and the poor condition of the bridge conspired to knock me off and I fell head over heels into empty space plummeting toward the rocks below. Just before I hit the rocks, I woke up.

I sat upright in bed and tried to catch my breath. I'm not prone to nightmares, in fact I rarely recall my dreams at all, but that one scared me into a cold sweat. I looked around the room to confirm my surroundings and assure myself that I was out of the dream. Jenna was asleep next to me, her rhythmic breathing undisturbed by my sudden jerk. Dawn was nearing but I felt as if I hadn't gotten an ounce of rest so I laid back and stared at the ceiling, trying to decipher the meaning in the dream. I was still puzzling over it when sleep returned, this time quietly.

When I woke, Jenna was already up, having a cup of room service coffee, and looking out the window on the early morning city.

"I see why you like this time of day," she said once she noticed I was awake. "It's the quiet time before the rush of people hit the streets. Even here, where people are going all night. The calm before the storm."

She poured me a cup of coffee and I joined her at the window. I slipped my arm around her waist and pulled her close to me.

"Did we really do what I think we did, Tory? Was it a dream?"

"Look at your finger," I said. "Is that band of silver a dream?"

"I've been looking at it all morning. Every time I do, I start to cry."

And to prove her point her eyes teared up and she put her head against my shoulder, sobbing lightly.

"I can't tell you how much you mean to me."

She didn't have to. I knew how much she meant to me and if her feelings were only half of my own, I knew how deeply I was loved. After all, what is half of infinity?

The breakfast platter was scattered with pastries of various types. I grabbed a croissant and pulled it in half, putting part of it in her mouth and part in my own. I wiped the crumbs from her lips and then gave her a gentle kiss.

"Those are good," she said through a mouthful of pastry.

"There's a place in Chicago that makes great croissants." I told her. "We should go there."

"California first. I want to see those trees you told me about."

Her face lit up with that glorious smile. I held her close and together we watched the desert wake up.

We spent that day away from Bernie and Denny. They said they were going to explore on their own and give us honeymooners some time to ourselves. It was strange being without them. In the short time we had been together, we had all grown so close. Neither of us could imagine being away from them but we both knew that our path led to California, while theirs led back east. Just the thought of that reminded me that we still had miles of desert to cross before we got to the green forest of California. We would need to figure out how we were going to get there.

Bernie and Denny were leaving on Saturday. They were going to head back to Kay's in Vail before making the long trek back home. We decided that Saturday would be as good a day as any for us to resume our own journey west. We still had a significant amount of money left from our first night winnings, so we purchased a pair of tickets for a bus bound to Bakersfield. Once we got there we would decide how to get north to Sequoia National Park.

We spent the rest of the afternoon sunning ourselves by the pool and playing video games in the casino arcade. Bernie and Denny showed up around dinnertime and we ate and drank and danced until bed called and we all returned to our rooms.

I awoke that night to a horrible hacking sound from the bathroom. Jenna was coughing again, but this time she was vomiting as well. Between coughs and heaves, she moaned in pain. I rushed to the bathroom to see if I could help.

She sent me out for some antacid and cough drops. Before I left I woke Denny and asked her to stay with Jenna until I got back. There was nothing open in the hotel so I had to trek down the strip to an all-night convenience store. When I got back, Jenna and Denny were laying on the bed. Jenna was asleep with her head resting on Denny's shoulder. Denny's arm held her close.

"What's wrong with her Tory?" Denny asked. Her eyes were filled with concern. "I've never seen anyone get so sick unless they were completely drunk. She didn't drink that much tonight."

"I know," I replied, not knowing if I should spill the beans about Jenna's condition. "She was coughing pretty fiercely. Maybe all the coughing made her gag."

Denny looked at me suspiciously. I knew my dodge had failed but I kept my mouth shut.

"She needs to see a doctor, Tory. She was spitting up blood."

Although I didn't need any coaxing, the sound of that was enough to scare me into agreeing to take her to a doctor in the morning. I thanked Denny for her help and told her I would take care of Jenna until morning.

I laid awake for the rest of the night, struggling with my conscience again. Jenna needed treatment for her condition and I was blindly carrying on as if she didn't. She was as guilty as I was. She knew what needed to be done and had decided against it. Once again I wondered exactly how much time we would have together.

The desert sun rose on a beautiful Friday morning without so much as a hint of an answer to the questions that swarmed in my mind. Jenna was lethargic that morning. She wouldn't get out of bed, even when she was wide-awake. She just lay on her side, surfing through the TV channels. Her eyes were glassy and her color was horrible. A few faint splotches appeared around her mouth. I tried to get her to eat, to get up and go to the doctor, to do anything, but she flatly refused. Denny and Bernie offered their recommendation that she see a doctor. I think that if they had known what was wrong with her, they would have been more adamant. As it was, I was left on my own after promising them that I would get her up and moving. By 2:00pm, however, I was so utterly frustrated that I went down to the hotel nightclub to drown my sorrows.

A young comedian was on the small stage at the far end of the room. His jokes were fair but his delivery was poor. He made me think of Officer Jimmy Bolton – the "stand-up" patrolman back in Kansas. I think Jimmy's delivery would have been better.

I reminisced over a pitcher of beer for an hour or so, thinking about how far we had come in the two weeks we had known each other. It seemed so long ago. I thought about all of the people we had met and the things we had talked about. I thought what a horrible joke it would be if all of this living and loving were over in a flash, like a match that burns out just after the initial flare.

I watched the comedian, trying to make his way, to fulfill his dream, and I suddenly thought about Jenna's "To Do" list. One of the items on that list was to sing on stage in a nightclub! This comedian was obviously no professional so I asked the bartender, a man named Reuben James (yep, just like the song!) if anyone could take the stage and perform. He told me that afternoons were generally amateur hour and if I could clear it with the club manager, I could do whatever I wanted on stage, short of stripping.

I found the manager, a heavyset man who introduced himself simply as Gorby. I suspect that his nickname came from a similar birthmark on his forehead to that of the former Soviet leader. I asked him if the stage was free around 4:30. My intention was to lure Jenna out of the room with the promise of fulfilling one of her wishes.

"What's your act?" Gorby asked as he puffed on a filterless cigarette, pausing periodically to spit a straggler of tobacco on the floor. He reminded me very much of Harlan.

"My wife and I are a musical duet. I play. She sings."

"What kind of music?" He asked through a harsh cough.

"Variety. Folk. Pop. Nothing outrageous. I play the guitar – acoustic – and she sings."

"Original stuff?"

"Some."

"Gotta be careful around here with that original stuff. There's a lot of people hang around these places hoping to swipe a song or two, especially when their own music's run dry."

"Well, I could play something popular, then. Let them steal someone else's music, right?"

"Damn straight. You ain't as stupid as I look, kid. Ok, you're on at 4:30. Good time slot, too. Night crowd starts drifting in. You should have a decent audience."

I thanked him and returned to the bar to clear my tab.

"Did you get a booking?" The bartender asked.

"Yes," I replied, paying for the beer and sliding a five-dollar bill under my glass as a tip. "We'll be back at 4:30."

He wished me well with a wink and slipped the five into the tip jar. I left the club and returned to the room.

At first Jenna wanted nothing to do with my plan. I told her that I was tired of seeing her lie around feeling sorry for herself. I told her that I thought I had married a woman who wanted to live each moment of her life to the fullest. I told her a lot of things. Most designed to make her angry.

It wasn't until I took out her journal and began thumbing through the pages reading off her wish list that she got angry and stomped across the room to snatch it away from me. I held it up out of her reach but she did me one better by delivering a well-aimed rabbit punch to my mid-section, effectively knocking the wind out of me. I lay on the floor for a few minutes with my knees pulled up to my chin, trying to synchronize my breathing. I must have been a pathetic sight as she was soon on the floor next to me, apologizing through a flurry of kisses.

"You're a shit," she said. "A real shit. For taking my book. For being mean. But mostly for being right."

I held her close as we lay on the floor. We didn't get up for several minutes. We just stayed on the floor holding each other. I put her in the shower to get ready for the show. While I was scrubbing her back, I saw that a few splotches had appeared just above her left hip. They were a bit darker than the ones near her mouth, which seemed to have faded somewhat. I didn't mention them, however, as I didn't want to depress her. I had very strong feeling that they were related to her condition.

Why do I keep referring to it as "her condition" or "her disease?" Why can't I just write the word? AIDS! AIDS! AIDS! AIDS! Why do I have to be so damn diplomatic about such a ruthless killer? I'm sorry for sounding so angry, but I am. I'm very angry. It angers me that someone so innocent and young was condemned to die through no fault of her own.

I'm sorry for that. Periodically my grief, frustration and self-pity reach critical mass and I need to vent. I just want this nightmare to be over for everyone affected.

So anyway...

We took the stage at 4:30 sharp. I left a note on Bernie's door inviting the two of them to the performance. They showed up about half way through our 45 minute set.

We played small sets of Beatles and Eagles tunes and intersperse a variety of other songs as well. Erik managed to stay in tune throughout the set. I chimed in on a few songs providing harmony where appropriate. It felt great to be up there with her.

Jenna sang like a professional, as if she had been performing her entire life. I provided her with written lyrics to all the songs I thought would work. She insisted that I slip in *Buyin' Time* as well. When she sang my song it was as if it had been written for her voice. I knew that I wanted to hear her sing some of my other numbers.

The crowd grew a bit while we performed. People filtered in and out of the club, but more in than out.

Eventually we were performing to an audience of about fifty, including Bernie and Denny. At the end of each song, we were rewarded with a warm applause. It was better than I expected and more than Jenna had ever hoped for.

When we finished our set with an encore of *Buyin' Time*, Jenna told the crowd that it was an original number hoping, she told me later, that a representative of the recording industry was listening. Her hopes were unfulfilled.

After our set, we met up with Bernie and Denny and had our last dinner together. During the meal Jenna told them everything. They sat quietly and listened to the story of the car accident, the blood transfusion, and her decision to live life at high speed rather than waste way with a tube plugged into her arm. She told them about the journal and her "To Do" list. I kept my mouth shut and moved food around on my plate with my fork. I couldn't seem to eat anything.

When she finished talking, Jenna returned to her meal. Denny was crying. Bernie was silent and sullen, his face buried in his hands. It was the longest silence we had experienced since the sighting of the phantom hitchhiker in the desert. Finally Denny broke the silence.

"Are you infected as well, Tory?"

"No," I said, although I truly didn't know.

"Are you sure?" She asked.

All I could manage for an answer was a shrug.

"We've been careful," Jenna offered. "There was only one time that we weren't."

"That's all it takes, Jenna!" Denny snapped.

Jenna sat upright and anger lit her eyes. She was about to tear into Denny for being so abrupt, but Denny realized what she had done and apologized.

"What a mad fucking world," Bernie said from behind his shaking hands. He dropped them to the table and all three of us saw that he had been quietly crying. "A completely mad fucking world."

"Well," I said, trying to change the subject. "Tonight is our last night together. I say we stay up all night and party like there's no tomorrow."

The quiet returned to the table. My stab at lightening the mood only managed to point out that we would soon be parted from our new friends. I managed to change from one sad topic to another.

"Indeed," Bernie said at last, relieving some of the burden of guilt from my shoulders.

"We never really had a wedding reception," Jenna said.

"I want to get a tattoo," Denny offered. Her comment was so unexpected that we all broke into laughter and the mood finally began to pick up.

"That's my sweet, delicate Denise. Tattoos, leather whips and chains. My own personal biker mama!"

"Piss off," Denny replied. "Pardon my German."

I don't recall the German translation that Bernie offered, but with that short exchange of multi-lingual vulgarity the evening began.

We didn't gamble at all that night, choosing instead to spend our money on food, drinks, and cover charges at nightclubs. We danced everywhere we went. We toasted friendship, true love, the bliss of marriage, and the beauty of karma. We ate things that we would never have eaten on any other night including, I think, something made from cow's stomach, and a variety of eel dishes.

Denny got her tattoo – a small rosebud over her heart with an inscription beneath that said, *Tory and Jenna were here*. She had to open her shirt to show us the final product. Her modesty had been virtually erased by a large quantity of vodka. I can only say that it is fortunate that we were out on the street and not in the middle of a crowded nightclub when she chose to show it off!

At the last dance club, Bernie and Jenna went out on the floor. Denny told the DJ that we were having a mini-reception and bribed him to play *Daddy's Little Girl*. I wish it could have been you dancing with her, Dad. Bernie made a fair stand-in. I got very misty-eyed watching them, and when the song ended the entire dance floor applauded them.

We lived that night like a pack of vampires, racing to do as much as we could before the sun peeked over the Eastern horizon. But when dawn inevitably came we found ourselves on the outskirts of town, sitting, and in some cases lying, on the hard dry ground. We all held hands as the sun rose and painted the morning sky.

"Well," Bernie said at last. "I suppose we should get you two checked out of the hotel and onto your bus."

That was the last significant thing any of us said until we were standing at the bus station.

"Do you realize that we've only known each other for nine days?" Denny asked.

"Feels like a lifetime," replied Jenna.

"And now it's over."

"It's not over," I said. "We'll still know each other after today."

"True enough," Bernie said. "But will we see you again?"

"Of course," I answered with a smile. But something inside me told me I was wrong. Things were going to change as soon as we got on that bus. Maybe not right away, but they were going to change.

The bus driver called for us to board. The finality of the moment was overwhelming. We hugged and kissed and made promises we probably couldn't keep. I made sure that Bernie still had the drawing of Jenna and me. Denny made me promise to get Jenna to a doctor and made Jenna promise that she would go. They gave us an open invitation to visit them in Illinois. And then we were on the bus and gone.

David Telford

March 26 – Still in Memphis

Got to Graceland today. I thought it fitting since I was still reminiscing about our crazy wedding in Vegas. Got to see the original suit that Jenna's costume was modeled after. I did my best to fight back the emotions until I got outside again. I'm sitting in a blues club right now, finishing off a little BBQ and trying to regain my momentum on this crazy long letter. Things start getting difficult from here, not that they've been easy up until now. Onward.

Jenna was asleep before we were too far out of town, exhausted from our all-night party and the emotional stress of the farewell. I moved to a seat across the aisle and let her stretch out over both of our seats. I set Erik in the next seat to me and stuffed my rucksack, containing my new clothes and the remainder of our money (about $1500) under the seat in front of me. The man in that seat turned and gave me a smile. I smiled back but didn't initiate a conversation. Something about the look in his eyes unsettled me. Besides, I was as worn out as Jenna. So instead I curled up in the corner of the seat and watched the desert pass by the window. Before I knew it I was in dreamland myself.

After what seemed only a few minutes, the bus driver

was shaking me awake, telling me that we had arrived in Bakersfield. The bus was empty except for Jenna and me.

"You two need to purchase a ticket to Los Angeles if you want to stay on," he said.

"No," I replied. "This is where we're going."

I woke Jenna and slowly we got ourselves together.

I retrieved my pack from under the seat and when I pulled some of my belongings rolled out on the floor. The drawstring on the top flap was hanging loose and the flap was hanging open. I never leave it that way but thought that perhaps in my exhaustion I had neglected to tie it. Nevertheless, when we got off the bus I made quick search of my pack to see if anything was missing.

My suit and our money were gone. Someone had stolen them while we slept. All I could remember was the smiling passenger with the strange eyes. I couldn't believe that I had been so stupid to leave that much money in an unsecured rucksack while I slept amidst a busload of strangers. Stupid!

Jenna sat down and checked her own pack. Her dress was still inside and she had about $40 stuffed in the pocket of a pair of cut-off jeans. She began to cry.

"What are we going to do?" She asked through her tears.

I was more upset about the suit than the money. I had enjoyed having money but I was used to living without it. I think Jenna had gotten used to the brief high-life we had. I did my best to console her, to assure her that the loss of the money meant only a return to the way we were living before we met Bernie and Denny.

But I mourned the loss of the suit. I doubted that I would have many opportunities to wear it, and it simply added to the amount of things I had to carry with me, but it was a symbol of our wedding and our time with our friends. It was a monumental loss.

Eventually we gathered our belongings and struck out to find something inexpensive to eat. I told Jenna that we should try to save the cash we had left, and look for a place that will let us work off a meal. She insisted that we buy our food this time so we could relax, eat and plan our trip north.

We settled on a couple of $1.99 breakfast specials at a nearby diner. While we ate we looked over my faded, dog-eared AAA road atlas. We decided to head toward Sequoia National Park and see the enormous trees there before striking out for Yosemite. I told Jenna that I'd like to show her San Francisco, so we planned our journey that far and postponed any further plans until we had taken in as much of the ocean as we could stand.

The meal and the plans helped to pick up our spirits. The loss of the money was now only an inconvenience, although I still felt a twinge of grief when I thought about the suit. I still do.

Before we started out, I posed some very serious questions to Jenna about her health. I told her that I wanted her to see a doctor immediately. She argued that she felt fine, but I managed to get her to promise to see one when we got to San Francisco. Then with the check paid, and the change left for a tip, we shouldered our gear and struck out for Sequoia.

As we walked along the highway I played Erik and

sang a few of my other tunes, while Jenna's narrow thumb saluted the passing cars. The weather was beautiful, not too hot with a light breeze blowing, so I didn't mind that most of the cars drove by without even slowing. Most of them were tourists anyway, and there is usually very little extra space in a tourist's car.

After a few miles of walking, and a second round of my songs, an 18-wheeler slowed down and pulled to the side. Jenna and I ran up to the driver's side of the cab and thanked him for stopping. The man behind the wheel returned our greeting with a smile unburdened by a great many teeth. His tanned, weathered face poked out of the window over painted lettering that read *Jacques "Crawdaddy" Boduin, Grand Bayou, LA*.

"Ha y'all are?" He called down from the cab.

"Great!" Jenna replied. "How's yours Crawdaddy?"

Once again, she was totally comfortable with dropping formality.

"Jes raht as rain, jolie. Y'all needin' a rahd?"

"Not too far," I said. "Just up to Sequoia. Is that where you're heading?"

"Hoo! Not far t'all. I goin' to make a pickup at the reservoir. Jump in!"

We scrambled around to the other side of the truck and climbed into the cab. The air conditioning was on and a Doug Kershaw tape was in an old but apparently reliable 8-track player. Next to the 8-track was a high-quality cassette deck and next to that a CD player. I found it interesting with that kind of high-tech equipment Crawdaddy preferred the sound out of his 8-track.

He asked how Jenna happened to know his name. She told him it was painted on the door.

"Aw man, I fo' got 'bout dat. My son, Lemont, he had put dat dere."

"You're a long way from home," Jenna said.

"Dat's for true. Been out of Grand Bayou near a year. Came out of dere with my son. He say, 'Crawdaddy we got to move to California. Make some money out dere.' Well, here I are."

"So you live here now," I added.

"Yessir. Livin' in Los Angeles."

When Crawdaddy talked about Los Angeles he pronounced it *Laiz Onzhell*, but I'll continue to spell it the 'raht' way.

We chatted it up with Crawdaddy for a few miles then he reached over and popped the 8-track out of the player.

"Play some on that gee'tar, son."

I responded with a slightly out of tune version of *Born on the Bayou*. Surprisingly, or maybe not, Crawdaddy knew the song and sang along putting the duet even more out of tune, I'm afraid. When we finished Jenna jabbed me in the side and whispered, "And you thought *I* couldn't yodel."

We sang a few more tunes and then popped the Doug Kershaw tape back in the player. I managed to strum through some of the chords accompanying the ferocious fiddle riffs and was soon able to play along. Crawdaddy started singing again. Jenna just stared out the front window with a long grin on her face. She was enjoying the ride but she was right, Crawdaddy could not sing.

Correction – he could sing, just not in tune.

In the town of Lake Isabella we parted company with Crawdaddy. We thanked him for the ride and songs. He said that it was his pleasure and recommended I tune up my gee'tar. Jenna commented as he pulled away that he must have no idea how tone deaf he is. I agreed.

We had a little over $30 left, which I wanted to save, but Jenna insisted on buying some food to take into the forest with us. I argued that we would be better off saving it and working for a meal. She countered my position by stating that she doubted there were any diners in the forest for us to work at. She then walked into a grocery store and left me on the sidewalk. In the end I was glad she was so stubborn as we were several miles into the park when we got hungry.

We mostly kept to the main trails wandering only a little when something off the trail caught our eye. The trees were incredible. Unless you've been in the midst of an old growth forest you can't comprehend the depth of spirit in the trees. The forest was overflowing with energy. It was like wading through pure spirit. Jenna and I both felt it and talked about it as we walked. Together we developed a theory that trees must be the highest form of life. They find what they need whether it's water, nutrients, or sunlight, and push ever upwards. They do this while maintaining a sense of peace about them. In fact, if there was ever a true symbol of peace I think it would more likely be a tree than a dove.

We strolled through the shade of the canopy, hugged a few of the enormous trunks, and made love on the soft moss that blanketed the ground. The entire time we spent wandering the trails we saw very few other people, mostly other hikers and always off in the distance. It was as if we had that whole section of forest to ourselves.

We camped near a clear stream and built a small fire to cook the hotdogs and potatoes Jenna had bought. After dinner we combined our bedrolls and curled up to go to sleep. Our conversation slackened, not because we didn't have anything to say, but more because nighttime in a place like that deserves a certain kind of reverence. It was like being in church.

Early in the morning, about an hour or so before dawn, I was awakened by a splashing sound coming from the stream. I was startled a bit thinking it might be something like a bear or cougar. As my eyes grew accustomed to the darkness I saw the outline of four large animals wading down the stream past our little camp. It was a small group of deer or elk or something. In the pre-dawn gloom I could only tell that they were some kind of deer-like creature.

I gave Jenna a little shake and clamped my hand over her mouth just before she gave a shout. I pointed to the stream. The four animals stood upright and alert in response to her stifled cry. The leader, an enormous buck with a fabulous crown of antlers looked directly in our direction. We remained there, the four of them and the two of us, motionless, sizing each other up for two or three minutes.

Then, as if he decided we were nothing more than logs, or just that we were harmless to him and his harem, the big buck continued his slow stroll upstream taking periodic sips of the cold water.

We remained quiet until the sound of their splashing was far in the distance.

"That was incredible," Jenna whispered.

"Yeah."

"I thought he was going to charge at us."

"He might have," I said. "Did you see the antlers on him?"

"Those were antlers? I thought he'd strapped a dead tree to his head."

We giggled and held each other, still feeling the thrill of the close encounter with such a powerful creature.

"I love you," she whispered, her lips brushing against my cheek as she spoke. "I have seen so many things because of you."

I kissed her and pulled her even closer.

"So have I."

We made love again, this time I'm afraid as unprotected as the first. It was as if we had forgotten the danger involved. Afterward, we lay on our backs looking up through the canopy of trees watching the morning slowly paint the night sky with a pallet only God could wield. I realized at that point that I had been seeing the world as if it had been drawn with plain graphite pencils – like a living representation of my own drawings. Because of Jenna, the world I see now is alive with colors.

I sat up and retrieved the notebook from my pack. I closed my eyes and felt *him* come to the surface. The pencil danced across the page. When I finished, I read the poem that had poured out of the emotions I was feeling.

> *As dreams sweep through your sleeping mind,*
> *And dawn delays its morning wash,*
> *I look upon your form and find*
> *The places last I dared to touch.*
>
> *The graceful curves along your hips.*
> *The shade below your supple breast.*
> *The corner of your ruby lips,*
> *Where strands of hair have set to rest.*
>
> *Your gentle hand, your rounded heel,*
> *The softness of your graceful nape.*
> *A thousand places still to feel*
> *In reverence of your wondrous shape.*
>
> *But night continues toward the dawn*
> *And drives the silver westering moon.*
> *At last to sleep I shall succumb*
> *To wake, to touch you, tomorrow, soon.*

Jenna responded by tearing the sheet of paper out of the notebook, haphazardly folding it, and then putting it in her own pack.

"Thank you, again."

We washed ourselves in the cold stream, sitting naked on the smooth stones that lined the bottom and letting the crisp current sweep around us. It was invigorating. Jenna rinsed out the empty soda container from the previous day's hike and filled it with the cool water.

After the bath, a quick breakfast, and an all too brief period of photosynthesizing, we packed up our camp and continued our trek into the park. We hiked on and on until we came to a road. We intended crossing and continuing with our hike, but a sign on the westbound lane caused us to change direction. The sign read: Woody 14.

Jenna stared at the sign as if she were seeing some secret message buried in its rusting surface.

"Well," she said very matter-of-factly, "I guess we owe it to our friend to find out how his town is doing!"

"I guess so," I replied and we were off.

"What about the fourteen?" I asked. "Is that significant?"

"Fourteen? On the sign?"

"Yes."

"Well, fourteen is two times seven and seven is a magic number. There are two of us so that makes seven for each!"

"I thought it might refer to a date. Yesterday was the fourteenth."

"So it was."

We fell silent again, taking in the scenery as we trekked toward Woody. I thought she had forgotten about the numbers, but after a few miles she broke the silence.

"I bet there were fourteen points on that deer's antlers. Seven on each side."

"He was magnificent, wasn't he?"

"No, he was beautiful. You are magnificent."

I blushed and was about to respond with my own burst of flattery when she finished her thought.

"You're not beautiful. Magnificent? Yes! But you're one butt ugly man, Angus."

With that she burst into a sprint and ran down the road laughing at her own wit. I shouted and chased after her. She could very easily have outrun me but she slowed and let me catch her.

"You're a strange piece of work, Mrs. McLeod," I said, holding her tightly. "Kiss me."

"You want me to kiss that?" She said pointing at my mouth and making such a sour face that for a moment she might have convinced me that she was serious. But her grimace faded into a laugh and she responded to my request.

"I like that. 'Mrs. McLeod.' I love you Tory."

We hugged each other for a long time before continuing on.

Woody was nothing special, discounting its proximity to Sequoia. It was another town in another place. The destiny we hoped to find waiting there had either left without us or gotten lost on its way to meet us. Either way we wandered into town with our measly possessions (no offense to Erik!) and about $13.00 in our pockets. It was time we worked for a meal.

We struck out at the local diner, passed on the chain stores and even tried to convince the manager of the local hardware store that we could perform a pretty fair inventory if she was in the need. We ended up hungry and dejected on the curb outside the *7-11*.

"I suppose stripping is about all we could do to raise

some money in this town," Jenna said, watching the cars pass by. I thought she was kidding until she added, "That's not a bad idea!"

"What? You can't be…"

"How do you look in pasties?" She added, capping off the joke with a perfectly timed punch line.

I laughed and returned to my thoughts.

Parked alongside the convenience store were a couple of beautifully customized Harleys. The paint on the tanks and fenders was incredibly detailed depicting a southwestern desert scene complete with soaring eagles, a lone Indian with his horse, and the inevitable sun-bleached cow skull. The Maestro suddenly wanted out.

I took out my new pad and the colored pencils and began working on the first bike. Jenna offered some vague comment to the timing of my drawing session but left me to my own. The motorcycle rose from the paper, custom paint and all. I had to sharpen my pencils several times in order to capture the detail, but in the end, the paper contained a very close representation of the big Harley.

I scratched my signature in my customary spot and rolled back the paper to allow me a fresh canvas to sketch the other bike. Just as I was about to begin I felt a tap on my elbow.

"What?" I said, rather nastily. The Maestro doesn't like to be interrupted.

She pointed up above my head. I looked up into the face of a biker about the size of Montana. His eyes were hidden behind reflective sunglasses and his face was covered with a thick beard. His hair hung down beneath his leather hat, which along with his jacket, was painted in a similar style to the gas tank and fenders of the bike I had just drawn. I hadn't heard him walk up behind me.

The Maestro retreated almost immediately.

"That's pretty damn good, junior," the mountain of leather and hair said through a deep raspy voice. "You gonna draw the other one?"

"Thought I would," I said, still looking up, straining my neck. "Is that all right?"

"Shit yeah!" He replied. "You gonna let me buy them off you?"

Jenna tapped me on the shoulder, letting me know that she had something to say. I must have been hypnotized by the size of the man as she followed up a few moments later with a pretty hard punch.

"Uh, you'll have to talk to my manager," I said, never taking my eyes off my reflection in his sunglasses.

"That you?" He asked, waving a bottle of apple juice at Jenna.

"That's me big fella," she replied as she stood and held out her had. "Jennifer Baines McLeod. My friends call me Jenna. You…Well, you can call me whatever you want. What am I going to do about it right?"

The man laughed and took Jenna's tiny hand in his enormous one.

"Rushmore," he said with a grin. "Just call me Rushmore."

"Fitting," she replied. "Well, Mr. Rushmore…"

"Just, Rushmore."

"Ok," she said with that beaming smile that lit up her

entire face. "Rushmore. This is my husband, Tory."

"Pleasure," he said reaching down and engulfing my hand in his own. I was reminded of Harlan although I had a feeling this man could overshadow even that big Kansan. Don't get me wrong. He wasn't fat. He was just big. Athletic but big. Really big.

"He's the artist. I'm the deal maker," Jenna continued.

"I see."

"We've just come out of Sequoia, on our way north, and have found ourselves a little light in the pocket. We'd be happy to sell this picture..."

"Where are you heading?"

A new voice was added to our conference. We all turned to look toward the source of the voice, a man as narrow as Rushmore was wide, but just as tall. He was also covered in leather with paintings that matched the ocean scenery covering the other Harley.

"Stinger," Rushmore called. "You should see the drawing this guy did of my bike. He's about to do yours."

Rushmore introduced us to his friend. Stinger looked over the drawing while Jenna continued the bargaining.

"We were just on our way up to Yosemite, but as I told your monumental friend here, we are a little low on cash."

"Probably hungry too, huh?" Stinger interrupted without looking up from the drawing.

Jenna looked at me, silently asking if she should answer.

"I could eat," I offered.

"We could stand for a bit of food, yes," Jenna replied returning her gaze to the two bikers.

"Me too," Rushmore added.

"Big shock there," Stinger quipped, throwing a sideways glance at his big friend. "So, let's eat. We'll talk business while we munch."

"A business lunch," Rushmore declared.

"Tax break!" They both shouted in unison.

Jenna gave me a scowl as if to say, *What have we stumbled upon here!?*

I picked myself up off the curb and the four of us walked to the diner that had previously turned us down for work. I was a bit uncomfortable going back in the place but I doubted that anyone inside would say anything to us considering the size and dress of our lunch companions.

Rushmore, Benjamin Rush, MD, is an endocrinologist in San Francisco. Stinger, Stephen Parker, is a tax attorney also in the Bay Area. Although we didn't discover it until much later, they were also, how do I say, *romantically involved*, and shared a huge house on Liberty Street. (I stayed with them for a couple of weeks after Jenna died. They were gracious, compassionate hosts and offered me a permanent room in their spacious digs, which I declined.)

The two took their vacations together and spent their time off bombing around the coast on their Harleys. Sometimes they hooked up with other weekend hog jockeys, but mostly they just rode together, enjoying California's plentiful sights and the time together that

Minstrel of a Modern Time

their hectic careers inhibited. Both of them are very compassionate caring people. Even Stinger the attorney! They are very active in the gay community in San Fran and contribute a large sum of money to AIDS research. Rushmore even donates his time in the AIDS clinics. Another of the many coincidences we encountered on our trip.

But anyway...

I packed away a BLT and fries trying to keep pace with Rushmore's enormous bites of his own thick sandwich. Jenna and Stinger talked business between bird-like bites of their own meals.

"The detail is fantastic," Stinger said, eyeballing the drawing from a distance of about 2 inches.

"It is," Jenna replied matter-of-factly. "He does extremely delicate work although you wouldn't know it to watch him eat."

Rushmore laughed and lost a piece of sliced turkey from his open mouth. I laughed in return and then gulped another mouthful myself.

"All right deary," Stinger said at least. "How much for this volunteer job, and how much to commission the other?"

Jenna nibbled a French fry and gazed out the window. After a few moments of mental calculation she asked me for a pencil. She wrote the amount on a napkin and slid it over to Stinger. Stinger took the quotation and held it up. Rushmore and I slowed our feast watching the two of them deal on these two minor pieces of art.

Stinger shook his head and scowled. Jenna looked a bit frantic and took a sip from her water glass as Stinger wrote his counter-offer and passed it back. When Jenna saw the bid Stinger had written she choked on her mouthful of water, spitting some of it out onto her plate. She held the paper up and gawked at it, and then back to Stinger who sat straight faced, waiting for her response. Rushmore returned to his meal smiling as if he knew Stinger's angle in these types of negotiations.

"You want to split another plate of fries, Tory?" He asked. I mumbled my assent through a mouthful of sandwich, and the order was called across the diner.

"Well?" Stinger prompted.

"That will be fine," Jenna replied, still choking on her water.

"Could you all excuse me? I need to use the restroom."

Stinger also excused himself for a similar cause. When they were both clear of the table, I reached over and read the writing on the napkin. Jenna's offer was on one side, crossed out by Stinger.

$100 each and you buy the meal

I flipped over the napkin and read the counter-offer. When I did I nearly choked on my own mouthful of food.

$300 each, the meal, and a ride to Yosemite.

I showed the napkin to Rushmore. He laughed.

"He likes to play that game. He lets a person make an offer and then he doubles it, or in this case, triples it.

He likes to watch the expression on their faces when they read a counter-offer better than their opening."

"It's too much," I said returning the napkin to its place.

"Not to us it isn't. It's excellent work. We take a lot of pride in those bikes. It's worth every penny. Probably more. Look at the money Warhol made painting soup cans."

"I've never sold anything before. I usually give them away."

"No wonder you're hungry," he said with a smile and a wink.

I sat silently while Rushmore mopped up a dollop of ketchup with a bundle of fries. His face suddenly became very serious.

"How sick is she?" He asked.

I was completely taken off guard. I had temporarily forgotten Jenna's illness, but Rushmore being a doctor had noticed almost immediately.

"I don't know," I replied, not even attempting to pretend ignorance. "She's had some bad days but for the most part she's been all right."

"If it's AIDS, she needs treatment."

"How did you know?"

"She has a few faded KS lesions on her neck and collar bone. She also looks a bit pasty but that could be malnutrition. I doubt you two eat very well or very often living the way you do, right?"

"What should I do? She doesn't want to see a doctor. I'm not qualified to handle this but I feel I should be doing something."

"Get her to a clinic as soon as possible. They'll put her on treatments – AZT most likely. In the long run AZT alone won't save her but it will help to prolong her life. Hopefully in the next couple of years we'll figure out a way to kill this thing. If we do, then we can save her."

"Where?"

"Bring her to San Francisco. I'll help you get her into a program."

"She won't go."

"Make her."

I quietly thought over the offer. Rushmore must have felt my frustration as he reached across the table and gripped my arm in support.

"What about you?" He asked.

"I don't think so."

"Are you using a condom?"

"Usually," I said, somewhat embarrassed.

"*Usually* isn't good enough, Tory. *Always* is your only option."

I couldn't argue with him. He was an expert on the topic. Besides, the little I did know should have been enough to scare me into abstinence. But I couldn't imagine not touching her. Not being with her for the rest of my life. But mostly I couldn't imagine being without her. The dilemma was agonizing.

"Listen," he said. "Go to Yosemite. Have some fun. Spend a few days slogging through the woods. Then come to me. I'll give you my address and number before we drop you off. You have to do this Tory. For both of you."

I agreed to get Jenna to San Francisco. I would figure a way to do it. She might hate me for tricking her into it, but somehow I would get her medical attention. Rushmore handed me a business card for the clinic where he volunteered which I slipped into my backpack just as Jenna returned from the restroom. Stinger followed a minute later.

The four of us sat quietly finishing our meal, offering only a few abstract comments about the food and the clientele of the diner. Stinger paid the check and we left for the Harleys.

Most of the day was behind us so we rode back toward Sequoia and camped again under the giant pines. Jenna told our new companions about the deer the night before. I took out Erik and managed a few soft songs before Stinger suggested we turn in. He wanted to be on the road early in order to drop us off at Yosemite before heading back to San Francisco.

David Telford

March 27 – Leaving Memphis

We woke to a glorious morning, perfect for riding. I rode behind Stinger, Jenna behind Rushmore. They insisted we wear the helmets they kept strapped to their saddlebags although they didn't wear helmets themselves. It was comical to see Jenna's tiny body snug behind the massive frame of Rushmore with his large helmet slipping down over her eyes. I gripped Stinger's waist and watched trees as we sped along the secondary roads heading north.

At one point Stinger decided to take the lead and passed Rushmore and Jenna. As we passed I caught Jenna's gaze. She looked euphoric. It was then that I heard for the first and only time her unspoken thoughts as they came into my mind. As clear as if she had spoken them into my ear I heard her say, *I'm riding a motorcycle! A Harley! Another thing to check off the list!* Then her gaze returned to the scenery and she gripped her enormous driver even tighter.

We stopped once for gas and another for a bathroom break but before we knew it we were driving up to the entrance to Yosemite National Park. Jenna dejectedly dismounted the iron horse and returned the helmet to Rushmore.

"How much time do you need?" Stinger asked,

referring to the drawing of his own motorcycle.

"I don't know, give me an hour or so," I said, although I figured I could do it in less time. I wanted to also do a quick black and white sketch of our two drivers – a little bonus for the ride.

"You go to it," he replied. "I'm going to go over in the sun and touch up my tan. All this leather makes me feel a little peaked. Jenna, darling, we have business to conclude."

"I'll go round up something to eat," Rushmore said as he remounted his machine. "Any requests?"

"Anything," I said.

"Nothing for me," Jenna replied.

"The usual," Stinger answered.

Without another word Rushmore sped off to the nearest source of junk food.

The motorcycle eased itself out of the paper. The Maestro had gotten used to the colored pencils and was now fairly adept at matching shades. While I was deep in the drawing, Rushmore returned with a large order from McDonald's. He set my meal next to me while I was working to refine the details of the ocean scenery painted on the tank and fenders of Stinger's ride. As I expected, I finished long before the time I quoted. I then opened up my new graphite pencils, which were still in the shrink-wrap, and began pulling the faces of the two bikers from a clean page. It took about twenty minutes to complete that drawing, and I scratched my signature just as the three of them approached.

"We couldn't wait," Stinger said. "Show me."

I showed him the sketch of the Stinger-mobile. He

smiled and sat on the ground next to me eyeing the detail while his head shook slowly from side to side.

"Perfect," he whispered.

Jenna had already accepted the money and showed me that we were now $600 richer with a subtle pat on the front pocket of her cut-off jeans. I tore off the two motorcycle sketches and handed them to their respective Harley owners. Then I tore off the third drawing of the two men and handed it to Rushmore. He looked at it for a minute ignoring the pleas of his companion to show him what I had drawn. Then he crouched down next to Stinger and slid his arm around the other man's shoulder as he held the picture out. It was at that moment that Jenna and I realized that there was more to their relationship than we had first guessed.

"This will go over our bed," Stinger said.

At first I was thrown by the words "our bed." I had never really developed a personal philosophy toward gay relationships. The narrow-minded upbringing I received in Columbia taught me that these relationships were abnormal and perverse, if not downright blasphemies against God and Nature. But these two didn't seem strange or unnatural. In fact, once I got to know them better, their relationship seemed as natural and comfortable as any heterosexual couple I have met. They loved and cared for each other. Nothing strange about that!

Jenna didn't seem to have a problem with the relationship between Stinger and Rushmore although I think she was as surprised as I was to finally recognize it.

We ended our time together over dinner. Rushmore

and I went head-to-head, or more appropriately, stomach-to-stomach, in another pig-out competition. Jenna and Stinger discussed the possibility of selling some of my work to a gallery owned by a friend of his in San Jose. We laughed and ate and bonded, until finally around 7:00pm the two bikers decided to head home.

"Come by and see us," Rushmore told Jenna, hiding the real purpose of his invitation. "When you're done here give me a call. I'll pick you up and bring you back to our place. You'll love San Francisco."

"We'll see," Jenna replied. "I think we're heading to Chicago next, but who knows? We can change our plans anytime we like. We'll talk about it."

"Well," he continued. "If you decide to go on to Chicago, call me anyway. I'll give you the name of a friend of mine up there. At least you'll have a roof over your heads while you're there."

"That would be nice. Thank you for everything Benjamin," Jenna answered with a sincere smile and a hug.

Stinger hugged us both and whispered something in Jenna's ear while they embraced. She smiled and nodded then said something quietly back to him. Some sort of clandestine arrangement regarding my drawings, I imagine although I never did find out. Rushmore shook my hand and passed me a piece of paper with the name of a doctor and clinic in Chicago.

"In case I don't see you again," he said.

I thanked him and slipped the paper into my pocket. Then with only a few more words, they were gone. We heard their hogs rumbling down the westward road for the next several minutes.

Jenna and I went into the park and hiked up to a campground where we rented a tent and campsite for the night. We lay together that night, wrapped in each other's arms, feeling good about making two more friends. Jenna was happy to have cash in her pocket again and promised not to be so reckless in how we spent it. I wanted to bring up the subject of her health but she dodged every attempt until I finally gave up and fell asleep.

She wasn't able to dodge the subject for long, however. I woke up sometime after midnight and she wasn't there. I left the tent, and made a beeline for the public restrooms hoping that she simply had to relieve herself. I found her sitting on the ground outside the building clutching her knees and rocking back and forth. She was crying pretty hard and didn't notice my approach.

"Are you all right?" I asked as I knelt beside her.

"Oh, Tory," she cried. "I'm so sick. My whole body hurts. God it hurts!"

It was then that I noticed that she had soiled herself. In addition, she had vomited and messed the front of her clothes as efficiently as she had the back. She was shaking and sweaty although she claimed that she was cold.

I told her to wait where she was. I ran back to our tent and tore into her rucksack to retrieve some clean clothes. I grabbed my blanket and took off back to the restrooms. As I passed another campsite, I noticed some beach towels hanging on a line, drying from the afternoon's swim I imagine. I snuck up and grabbed one of the big towels and ran back to Jenna.

I took her back into the ladies room hoping that we were alone, and turned on one of the showers. I removed her soiled clothes and stuffed them into the trashcan. I then put her in the shower, and washed away the mess that remained on her skin. I had to go to the sinks several times to get big handfuls of soap from the dispensers.

While I washed her I tried to get her to tell me what happened. Jenna stared like a zombie over my shoulder for nearly the entire shower. I couldn't get her to speak a single word until very near the end.

"I woke up with stomach cramps," she said finally. "I figured it was just my period, which is due, so I came here to take care of it, you know? I hadn't even gotten inside when I started throwing up. While I was on my hands and knees I started shaking and sweating. That's when the diarrhea came. I felt like my insides were going to explode."

"I need to get you to a doctor, Jenna. Enough is enough."

"No."

"Look, Rushmore works in an AIDS clinic in San Francisco…"

"You told him?" Her words were sharp with suspicion. "How could you do that?"

"I didn't. He's a doctor, for crying out loud!"

"Yeah, well how could he know I have HIV? You told him, didn't you?"

I pointed to the dark splotches under her arms and the faded ones near her neck.

"He saw these." I said. "He knows what they are."

Jenna looked at the marks on her side as if she was seeing them for the first time.

"Lesions," she said quietly.

"Yeah, that's what he called them. Lesions. Something like that. The point is, he knows about it and can help you."

"Nobody can help me, Tory. There's no cure, or haven't you been keeping up on things?"

I clamped my jaw tightly to keep from spouting out in anger and started to dry her off. But Jenna was venting.

"You're so intelligent and so worldly, but in some things you're a regular dunce, Tory. There is no cure! Got that! Nobody can help me! All they can do is prolong the inevitable. I don't want that! Are you listening?"

I stood up and threw down the towel. And then, as if a tidal wave of emotion crashed down on me, I went berserk.

"I am listening, God damn it! I *have* been listening! You don't want any help! You don't want to get better even if it's just for a month or a year or two! You want to be alive and then dead without a drawn out period of suffering! Have I got it right, Jenna? Have I?"

I kicked one of the stall doors in and pounded my fist on the metal partition.

"I get it!" I shouted. "Now you get this!"

I stormed out of the stall and stood face to face with her. Her own face was splashed with fear and surprise.

"You are all that I have! You are all that I want! So

don't you go and tell me all this selfish bullshit again! I want you to live! I want you with me! I want you to get some kind of treatment so that you can survive this monstrosity until a cure is found! I have listened to you hack and cough. I've stayed up with you while you threw up blood. Now I've cleaned puke and shit off you! I am in this until the end! I want you to be in it too! I can't fight it if you don't!"

At that point I broke down and cried. I don't know how long I sat there sobbing but under the stress I must have fallen asleep for a few minutes. When I finally looked up, Jenna was gone. I found her standing outside the door.

"You sleep in the ladies room often, McLeod?"

I was in no mood for her spontaneous wit. I turned from her and walked back to the camp. She followed but kept at a fair distance. I entered the tent and attempted to sleep. Jenna crawled in and kept to her own side. We didn't talk or sleep, the rest of the night. Jenna got up two more times to relieve the pain in her bowels. Each time I followed her and waited outside until she was finished and returned to the tent.

When morning came, I got up and went looking for breakfast. Jenna was dozing in her bedroll. The night had been hard on her physically and emotionally. I felt somewhat guilty for blowing my stack but I was becoming increasingly worried that I could lose her any day. I felt so out of control.

When I returned with breakfast, I heard Jenna moaning. I dropped the food and ran into the tent. She lay on her back, sweat running from her face. She had her bedroll pulled up tight as if she was freezing beneath the sheets. She was mumbling something about running away, and kept apologizing to you two. She was delirious. That was when I decided that enough was truly enough.

I ran to the rental office and told the teenager on duty to call an ambulance. I felt obligated to tell the paramedics that showed up about Jenna's condition. They were both very uncomfortable with the situation but managed to perform their duties professionally, albeit hesitantly.

Jenna was loaded onto the ambulance and put immediately on a fluid drip. The paramedics said that she was dehydrated and showed signs of malnutrition. I couldn't understand where the malnutrition came from as I had been carefully watching to see that she ate as regularly as possible. She told me later that she had been throwing up most of what she ate during the previous week. She had managed to hide it from me up until that night.

The ambulance took us to a small hospital not far from the park. I can't recall the name of the hospital or even the town it was near. The remainder of that day was a blur of doctors, nurses, tests, and forms. I found myself signing things that I had not even read. I'm sure some of them had to do with payment but I think the hospital staff knew that we would not be able to pay for the treatment she received.

Several specialists were called in, each assuring me that he or she would get Jenna on course for recovery. A few made sure I knew that there was no cure for her condition and that they could merely provide whatever care she required to see her through for now. All of them kept their distance – performing whatever tasks they had to as efficiently as possible and then exiting as if the mere sight of us was enough to infect them as well. I felt like a leper.

The worst part was that because of her semi-manic state of mind, they wouldn't let me into her room until they had finished their tests and had sufficiently sedated her. When I was finally allowed into the room she was out cold and attached to about a million dollars worth of machines.

I sat in a chair in the far corner of the room and watched her quiet steady breathing. I was completely disoriented. I knew that she needed to be in a hospital with whatever medication was necessary to see her through, but I couldn't help but feel that we were in the wrong place. We were supposed to be somewhere else but my frazzled mind couldn't remember where.

Sometime around dinner it came to me. I was gazing out the window looking at the hills and trees and felt the Maestro tickle me. I reached for my sketchpad and suddenly remembered Rushmore and his offer. I pushed the Maestro back and dug out the business card he offered me. Then I picked up the phone in Jenna's room and called the clinic, collect. The phone rang and rang and then an answering machine picked up and informed me that the clinic was closed for the evening and to call back between the hours of 9:00am and 5:00pm on the following day.

I hung up the phone and buried my face in my hands.

I didn't want to stay here. I wanted to be closer to Rushmore. He knew us. He didn't treat us like lepers. I needed to get to him or at least get Jenna out of this place. Perhaps a larger hospital would be better equipped to deal with our situation.

I called the head nurse into the room and demanded to see the doctor in charge of Jenna's case. She told me she would try but it was unlikely that the doctor was in the building. I told her I would wait. I had nowhere to go. She left unhappy with my attitude, I'm afraid, but fulfilled my request.

Dr. Mercedd was the specialist assigned to Jenna's case. He came into the room to deal with the "frantic young man" the nurse had reported to him. I told him that I was not frantic but concerned about the quality of care my wife would be receiving. I told him that I didn't like the "10-foot pole" treatment we were subjected to and requested that she be transferred to a facility where they had the expertise and compassion to deal with us.

Dr. Mercedd tried to convince me that his staff was more than qualified to handle Jenna's case and that I must allow for a bit of caution on their part as they were dealing with a contagious incurable condition. I stood my ground and demanded to be transferred or I would pitch such a fit in the hallways that I would make the other patients question the quality of the care they were there to receive. I threatened to write to the local papers to let them know just how chronically ill patients were treated at that hospital. I said all this with the poise, posture, and vocabulary of a lawyer. Speaking of which, I also threatened to call my attorney (Stinger!) and see that we were moved.

Dr. Mercedd stood silent, his jaw visibly clenched. He must have taken me seriously. He arranged for us to transfer to a larger hospital in Stockton, not quite San Francisco, but a bit closer. We had to spend the night where we were as our transportation was scheduled for the next day.

After the head nurse notified me of the transfer, I slumped back into my chair and put my feet up on the magazine table. I was exhausted, physically, emotionally, and spiritually. I leaned back and within minutes I was out cold.

March 29 – On the Road

Not sure where I'm going next. Probably spend Spring in the Adirondacks. I like it there when everything is greening. Spring cleaning in the northeast is cold hard work but there's usually a lot of work to be found so I should be able to keep busy and pad my pocket somewhat. But while I sit here with my coffee, I'll get back to the story.

A pretty young nurse offering coffee and doughnuts awakened me. She was the first person I had met in that place that treated me with any kindness. I thanked her for her offer and accepted on behalf of my growling stomach. Jenna was being prepared for transfer although she hadn't wakened yet.

The young nurse, Colleen, was from the hospital in Stockton. She was going to ride back with us and make sure that Jenna was comfortable on the trip. She sat with me and went over every line of the forms I needed to sign to authorize the transfer. I told her that I needed to get in touch with Dr. Rush in San Francisco as soon as possible. She assured me that we would be able to contact everyone we needed to.

By 10:00am we were on our way out. Colleen accompanied Jenna, who was still sedated, to the

Minstrel of a Modern Time

ambulance while I paid my final respects to the hospital staff and signed another ream of forms. I think they knew that the bill would be uncollectible but they insisted that each form be properly filled in. I must admit that on a couple of them I was a bit sarcastic, filling in the address section with quips like, *That depends on what day it is* and *Somewhere between Maine and Mexico.* Admittedly a bit childish but worth it, I think.

When I was done I joined my wife and her nurse in the back of the ambulance.

My first order of business once we got to Stockton was to contact Rushmore. Colleen located an empty office and told me to go ahead and dial direct. She doubted that anyone would question a call to another doctor. I'm sure that what she suggested was against hospital policy, but her willingness to risk something like that for Jenna and me showed a compassion for our situation not demonstrated at the other hospital. I felt that we were in good hands.

I didn't know what I would say when I finally heard Rushmore's voice on the other end. I rehearsed several greetings but my frazzled nerves made all of them sound exactly that – rehearsed. The phone rang twice before being picked up by a soft-spoken man. I asked for Dr. Rush and was put on hold. After 2 or 3 minutes of hold music, the man came back on.

"You're holding for Dr. Rush?"

"Yes."

"Can I tell him the nature of the call? Or your name, sir?"

"Tory."

"One moment."

Another minute of hold music and then Rushmore came on the phone. When I heard his voice, I lost it. I began crying uncontrollably, almost hyperventilating.

"Tory," Rushmore said calmly through the earpiece. "Get a grip, man. What's going on? Is it Jenna?"

"Yes," I managed to choke out. "We're in Stockton. She's sick, Rushmore."

"Stockton? Where?"

"I don't know. A hospital. St. Something or other."

"St. Joseph's?"

"Yeah, I think so. Rushmore? Can you come up here?"

"Yes. I can't come up until tomorrow so you have to hang on, all right? Listen, Tory, can you write this down? This is important."

I took out my notepad and a pencil.

"I want you to get in touch with Dr. Enzerillo at that hospital. Got it?"

I asked him to spell it for me.

"She's my counterpart at that hospital. Tell her you're a friend of mine and that I'll be coming up tomorrow. Got it?"

"Yes."

"I'm going to arrange for you to be transferred to my hospital. All right?"

"Yes."

"How's Jenna? What are her symptoms?"

I told him about the night before – the vomiting and diarrhea. I told him about the cold sweats and the delirious chatter. Rushmore listened carefully, interrupting only to verify a few minor details now and then.

"Ok," he said after I had explained everything as well as I could remember. "Hold tight, my friend. You're in good hands up there, but you'll be in better hands here. Stay with Jenna. Get in touch with Enzerillo. I'll see you tomorrow, ok?"

I thanked him and then hung up. I looked up and saw Colleen standing in the doorway.

"Dr. Enzerillo is on her way. I overheard your conversation. I hope you don't mind."

I thanked Colleen for being so patient and kind. I asked if I could go see Jenna. She led me into the room. Jenna was awake. I rushed to her side and wrapped my arms around her.

"Careful, McLeod," she whispered. "You're liable to unplug me."

"We wouldn't want that would we?" I laughed through tears.

"How do you feel?"

"No worse than you look, baby. You're still one butt ugly man."

I told Jenna all that had happened including the call to Rushmore. She was relieved that he was on his way and apologized for raking me over the coals when she found out that he knew about her.

"You were right," she said taking a sip of ice water to relieve the rasping in her throat. "I was selfish. I still don't want to suffer, but I'm willing to try to live a bit longer."

I thanked her. It seems I did a lot of "thanking" that day.

Colleen brought us both something to eat. Jenna was too weak to feed herself, and despite her sarcastic comments I fed her. After she ate she fell asleep.

Once again I found myself in a hospital room chair waiting for something to happen. At least I was content knowing that Rushmore was coming and that Jenna was in more compassionate hands. Dr. Enzerillo arrived while Jenna slept. She asked me a battery of questions regarding our lifestyle including our sexual habits. I answered them all even though I was uncomfortable telling her about our incidents of unprotected lovemaking. She didn't lecture me. She simply took the information and made notes.

I told her that I was a friend of Dr. Rush. She smiled when she heard his name.

"Well, then," she said. "If you're a friend of Ben's, you'll be well taken care of. And I'll wager that if there's ever a cure for this plague his name will be somewhere on the thesis."

Before she left she told me to let her know when Jenna woke up and suggested that I contact you two. It was the first time, I'm ashamed to say, that I had actually thought about getting in touch with you. I apologize for that. Still, I thought it best to wait for Jenna to take up and talk it over with her first.

Jenna woke up around 3:00pm. Dr. Enzerillo and another doctor came in and took blood and urine samples. They also checked her vital signs and questioned her about how she felt. When they were done, the other doctor left and Dr. Enzerillo took me aside.

"I would like to do some tests on you as well, Tory. Not necessarily for HIV, but I don't think that would hurt. Specifically, I'm looking for signs of a protozoan called *cryptosporidiosis*. The lab work sent up with Jenna shows signs of the oocysts." (I had Dr. E write down the name of the bug and the other technical jargon.)

I asked how she got it and how it could be cured.

"She got it from drinking contaminated water. Do you recall drinking out of a stream or creek that might have bordered farmland?"

I admitted that we had filled our water bottle in Sequoia, but I didn't recall any farmland nearby. I also told her about the deer and asked if they might have contaminated the water.

"It isn't likely. If the stream was moving fairly swiftly it's not likely the source of the problem. Still, pockets of still water could be a source and deer or other animals may carry the oocysts on their feet if they've walked through cow pastures. It's possible I suppose."

She continued by telling me that there is no real cure for the infection although she would try to ease the symptoms. Then I remembered skinny-dipping in Woody's pond. Dr. E said that was most likely the source especially if Jenna had swallowed some of the water.

"A person with AIDS," she said, "is going to have a hell of a time with this. We have to keep her hydrated and try to keep her digestive system working. I have to be honest. It's going to be ugly."

I told her that I would wait until I talked to Rushmore about everything. I was hesitant to submit to any tests. I was afraid of what I would find out. At that time ignorance was bliss. She agreed to wait and told me to let someone know if I displayed any of the symptoms of the crypto-bug.

I returned to Jenna and took her hand. I asked her how she felt and if I could get her anything.

"I could use a beer," she said.

By the look on her face, I could tell she was serious.

"No," I said. "I'm not going out to get you a beer."

"Why not?"

"For one, I don't think they would like you to have it. For another I don't want to leave your side."

"My hero," she said sarcastically.

"Stop it."

"Listen, I'm in a hospital, for crying out loud. I'm not going to die while you run down to the Stop-and-Shop and pick up a six-pack. Come on, Tory. A little party to celebrate our one week anniversary."

"A little late don't you think?"

"All the more reason to celebrate. Please?"

She kissed my fingers, which was the equivalent of twisting my arm. I agreed to try to sneak in some beer. I asked her if she wanted any chips and dip to go with it or perhaps some caviar.

"No one likes a smart ass, McLeod."

With that she rolled over and drifted off.

Rain clouds were rolling in as I quietly left the hospital. I was immediately reminded of that day when Jenna and I were caught in the downpour along that highway in Kansas, and the first time we made love. It seemed so long ago.

There wasn't a convenience store within a reasonable distance, but there was a bar. I went in and asked the bartender to sell me a six-pack of whatever brand he had in cans. He asked me for some ID, which of course I did not have. Instead I produced my wad of money and dropped a ten on the bar. The bartender looked at the bill and then at me.

"Doesn't look anything like you," he said, rousing a laugh from the regulars who lined the bar.

I picked up the ten and dropped a twenty. "Could be your father?" He said, initiating another round of laughs.

I picked up the ten and dropped a fifty. (Stinger had paid us with twelve $50 bills.)

"Oh, is that you?"

He produced a six-pack of Rolling Rock, and slid it across the bar. I thanked him for his fair business practice as I stuffed the beer in my rucksack.

"Oh no, thank you Mr. Grant! Or can I call you, Ulysses?"

The bar burst into laughter.

"A round of drinks on Mr. Grant," the bartender called as I left the building.

I returned to Jenna's room, having no trouble sneaking the beer in. She was asleep when I walked in but woke when I set the six-pack on the floor next to her. She seemed delighted that I had managed to purchase a brand from her home state. I popped the top on one of them and poured it into her cup. She sipped the beer through a straw, as she didn't have the strength to hold the cup to her lips.

"Now play me something," she said nodding toward Erik.

The rain began as I sat down and tuned up Erik. I thought it best to play something quiet since we were in a hospital. The Maestro came forward and the tune to a new song took shape on my fingers. I watched the rain spatter the windows as I played, hearing words form in my head to accompany the music. I kept them to myself. I was in no mood for singing.

Around 10:00pm, after two beers and several songs, Jenna fell asleep. I took advantage of the time to write down the words that were circling in my head. Those words and that new music turned into the song that I'm sending along with this letter. The recording is not that great so I'll include the lyrics below, so that you can better understand the mood of the moment.

> *I hear the drizzle of the rain.*
> *The memories all come back again.*
> *How we walked, arm in arm, hand in hand, and that man,*
> *A cigarette break on the balcony*
> *Looking down on our reverie*
> *As we danced in the rain.*
> *Oh the rain will never sound the same again.*
>
> *Did we drink far too many beers that night?*
> *Did we cry far too many tears?*
> *Did we say "Good-bye" or "See you soon" in that room?*
> *And as we embraced in the hall,*
> *Were our heads light from the love or alcohol?*
> *Well, I can speak for mine.*

That beer will never taste as fine, again.

Three weeks in June were all we had.
It's kind of sad, to think that hearts so young and free
Were parted before their chance to be full in bloom.
I never will forget those three weeks in June.

One last "Good-bye" that night in June.
We sat in silence under the summer moon.
If you had stayed would our love grow? I don't know.
But I think it would have been a crime
Had we not shared this precious time.
And I can tell you till my dying day.
My love for you will never fade away, my friend.

Three weeks in June were all we had,
But I'm glad, that we had the chance to say,
"I love you" in that special way. Aren't you?
I never will regret those three weeks in June.
I never will forget those three weeks in June.

I cleaned up the beer cans, rolled out my blanket on the floor and curled up for the night. Rushmore was coming in the morning. I had a feeling that things would be better once we got to San Francisco. I had a strange feeling, however, that we would never get there.

Colleen woke me the next morning. She greeted me with coffee, doughnuts and that sweet smile. Jenna was still asleep. I asked Colleen how she was doing. She said the chart showed that she was up twice in the night with violent cramping and diarrhea. The doctor on the night shift had given her some medication that was supposed to ease the cramps but it didn't seem to be working. I berated myself for sleeping through her agony.

I showered and changed into some clean clothes. I had been wearing the same shirt and jeans for two days and they had begun to smell a bit. Colleen took my dirty clothes and sent them to the hospital laundry – another taboo but she told me that the laundry manager owed her a favor so it wouldn't be a problem. I made a mental note to do a sketch for Colleen. Unfortunately, I never did it.

Rushmore arrived around 11:00am. I ran to greet him and find out what the game plan was. He looked strikingly different in a suit than in full length painted leather although he was still huge! The nurses and Dr. Enzerillo called him Ben, which is what he preferred when he wasn't riding his Harley across the countryside.

Ben shook my hand and told me that he was going to take me to lunch to discuss our options. He needed to consult with Dr. Enzerillo first and would come to get me, and check on Jenna when he was ready. I retreated to Jenna's room to wait.

Jenna was awake when I got there.

"Is he here yet?" She asked, with even less voice than the day before. She seemed weaker.

"Yes," I replied. "How are you feeling?"

"Numb."

"Did you sleep well?"

"Like a baby. Your guitar is like a lullaby."

Of course I knew she was lying and she was doing it to keep me from worrying.

"Good. I have a new song for you. I'll sing it to you tonight, ok?"

"Great. Are we leaving tonight?"

"Not tonight," Ben answered as he came into the room.

"Rushmooooooore," Jenna howled with a voice like a whisper.

"How are you princess?" Ben said with a big smile although his eyes betrayed the concern that lay just beneath the surface.

"Ready for another ride, big fella."

Ben laughed and took her hand.

"Soon enough. We have to get some weight on you and get your strength back."

"When do we go?" I asked.

"Tomorrow. I'm getting a private room for you with an extra bed so you can stay there too, Tory. I've lined up a good team of doctors, including yours truly, to help with this case. You may run out of drawing paper, Tory. I kind of leaked the word to them that you were something of an artist. They all have requests."

"I don't have a problem with that, as long as they'll take a drawing instead of cash."

"They will," he laughed.

"I'm taking your husband to lunch, princess. You get some rest and don't give the nurses or Dr. Enzerillo a hard time, got it? You're a stubborn woman, Jenna. That's how I know you're going to be all right."

I gave Jenna a kiss and then Ben and I went to the hospital cafeteria. We both ordered uncharacteristically light. Over lunch he talked to me about Jenna's condition and the severity of the crypto infection. He told me that I needed to prepare myself for anything because anything was exactly what could happen.

I told Ben the story of how Jenna and I met. I told him about the run-in with Arco and his gang, about the rain storm and the bridge, about skinny-dipping at Woody's, about yodeling in the Rockies, about Vegas and Elvis and the wedding. I told him about all of the people we had met including himself and Stinger, and how much they all played a part in this uncommon love story.

Ben listened to me rattle for nearly an hour, laughing at the humorous parts, frowning at the sad parts when I couldn't seem to fight back my tears. He was a perfect counterbalance to the mass of emotions that weighed on me. He kept me anchored and helped me clear away a place in my mind to prepare for whatever was to come.

As we walked to the elevator he put his hand on my shoulder.

"No matter what happens, Tory, you can stay with us. We have plenty of room for both of you."

"Is it likely that I'll be coming alone?" I was digging for Ben's honest opinion of Jenna's chances.

"To be honest," he said. "I think it's about 50-50."

His words struck me hard. It was what I wanted to hear – the truth. It was not the kind of truth I was looking for. I was hoping for better odds than a coin toss.

We returned to the room. Jenna was napping again. Dr. Enzerillo and Ben discussed the results of the latest samples and tests. They tossed around technical terms about "T cells" and a variety of other words ending in

-ase and –zine and other medical suffixes. I felt like a child whose parents spell words like "nap" and "bath." I couldn't understand most of what they said, but I think the gist was that Jenna was not responding to the medication used to fight off the cryptobug. Her condition was not getting better and Dr. Enzerillo was concerned that she might not handle the transfer very well. When they were done Dr. Enzerillo left and Ben sat down in the other chair.

"It doesn't look good, Tory. There are certain benchmarks we use to determine if a patient is recovering or failing. By those benchmarks, Jenna does not seem to be recovering, although she is not failing at a significant rate. I think we can turn this around but it's going to be a fight. Are you up to it? Emotionally, I mean."

"Yes," I said without thinking twice.

"Is she?"

"I think so. We should tell her everything when she wakes up."

"Tell me what," Jenna called softly from her bed.

"Tell you a riddle," Ben offered as if he had been prepared for her interruption.

Jenna perked up a bit and smiled in preparation for the riddle. I waited as well.

"Where in the world does one go to escape the world where one goes?"

Jenna repeated the riddle several times, memorizing it. I couldn't think of an answer off the top of my head but I had a feeling that it had something to do with our current situation.

"I'll be back in a little while," Ben said rising to leave. "See if you can come up with an answer by then, all right?"

Ben left me to explain to Jenna everything that was happening. I told her that we couldn't transfer her to Ben's hospital until she had significantly recovered from the crypto-bug. I also told her that they were concerned with her blood count and the lack of effect some of the medication was having on her. She took the news very matter-of-factly, as if I was talking about someone else. When I was done she laid silent for a while, stroking my hand with her narrow fingers.

"How are you?" She asked.

"I'm all right. I haven't shown any signs of the crypto thing."

"No, Tory. I mean how are *you*?"

She meant my emotional state. She meant how I was handling everything.

"It's hard," I said feeling my chin shake as the words left my lips. "Sometimes I'm strong, other times not. Sometimes I know we'll beat this thing and get you back on your feet. Sometimes I don't think we'll leave this room together."

"What does your heart tell you?"

"My heart? My heart hurts too much to speak to me. At times I feel overwhelmed by all that is happening. It's hard to believe that three weeks ago I was trying to swing a quick meal at Barb O's."

"Yeah, a lot has happened."

"Not enough. I want more. It's funny. I've survived for years on my wit and a smile. Erik's been my only companion for a long time. Then I met you and it seemed like all those years had been in preparation for that. Now when I think about possibly losing you, I feel so...lost. I can't imagine continuing without you."

Jenna squeezed my hand and pulled it up to her cheek.

"And what will we do if I live, Tory? Obviously I have to stop wandering the back roads. What will we do?"

I thought about it. I had not considered the fact that regardless of which way this battle went, her traveling days were over.

"Ben offered us some space at their house. I suppose I could take off my walking shoes and settle down for a while."

"I don't want you to do that," she replied. "It would be like caging a wild wolf. The road is your home. You need to wander. It's in your blood. You'd go crazy in the normal world."

"What about your parents? We could go there, right?"

"Yeah. I think that's where I'll go at least. You may want to go somewhere else but at least you'll know where to find me."

"I won't go anywhere else, Jenna. My home is with you now."

She kissed me softly and told me she loved me. I thought it was a good time to bring up you two. I asked her if I should call you and let you know what was going on. She told me to wait until we were in San Francisco.

"Daddy is too impetuous. He'd hop on the next

plane to Stockton only to find that we had moved to San Francisco. Let's get settled first."

I agreed to call you as soon as we were settled in San Francisco. The prospect frightened and exhilarated me. I couldn't wait to actually talk to you. But part of me was afraid, not knowing how to tell you who I was and why I was with your daughter. I decided to wait until I heard your voices before deciding how to explain the situation. Spontaneity! That's the ticket!

Ben came back and told us that he was heading back to San Francisco. He asked if we had come up with an answer to the riddle, which of course we had not. We promised to have an answer for him in the morning. He gave Jenna a kiss on the forehead and then left.

Jenna managed to stay awake through dinner and into the evening. We watched television and tried to work out the riddle.

Where in the world does one go, to escape the world where one goes?

We came up with several answers – to sleep, insane, an exit ramp, outer space. All of them were relatively correct but none felt right. We played other word games, asking riddles we remembered from our childhood, telling limericks and bad jokes. It was a nice quiet evening.

"Play me your song," Jenna said at last.

"Your song," I corrected, which forced a smile from her face.

I tuned up Erik and began to play. The words flowed

with the music better than I had expected. Jenna listened and giggled at the miscellaneous references to our experiences together. When I got to the part about saying "good-bye" she stopped giggling and closed her eyes. When I finished she opened her eyes and the smile returned.

"Beautiful," she said. "Play it again."

I complied and performed an encore. As I sang, she began to fall asleep. I put Erik quietly in the corner of the room and curled up next to her in the bed. I held her as sleep drifted in on her.

"Tory?"

"Yes, sweets."

"I'm going to go to the place where one goes to escape the world where one goes. Ok?"

"Ok, sweets. You go there."

"I'll see you later, McLeod."

"I'll be here, baby."

With that she fell asleep.

I held her for an hour or so, feeling the warmth of her body against me. She felt so thin, so fragile. I stayed in bed with her until the night nurse came in and told me I had to sleep somewhere else. She offered to bring a cot in for me but I declined, choosing to curl up on the floor again. It hadn't been a great day, but it had been a better one than the day before. The sun swung around to the other side of the Earth, preparing to rise again in a few hours, bringing with it the promise of better things. I fell asleep waiting for the sun to breach the horizon.

David Telford

April 2 – Cleveland, OH

Where in the world does one go to escape the world where one goes? One dies – that's where.

I've been avoiding this part for the past few days. I have to write it quickly to keep from breaking down so pardon my progressively sloppy handwriting.

Jenna died that night. It was the early morning of June 21. The infection of the cryptosporidiosis had spread too far for them to stop it in time. It allied with the KS lesions that had found their way to her intestines. Ben said that her waste removal system had collapsed, causing her blood to become toxic. She died in her sleep. She didn't suffer, as she feared.

I am suffering for her. I suffer the loss. The pain and torment she avoided exists ten-fold in my grief. I wonder if a person who dies in agony takes the burden of suffering from those who mourn. Is there some set level of misery to be endured in each passing – some through the process of dying, the balance by those who survive?

Ben came in around 7:30am. I had already discovered Jenna's passing. I sat on the floor with my face buried in the sheets and blankets of her bed, her narrow hand in mine. He knew as soon as he walked in.

"Tory," he said softly. "I don't know what to say.

Anything I can think of is insignificant."

"I know the answer to the riddle, Ben." I said wiping tears from my cheeks. "Jenna figured it out."

He thought about it and realized what I was trying to say.

"It's not the answer I was looking for," he said. "Certainly not the one I was hoping for."

I don't know why, but at that moment I had the desire to brush through Jenna's hair. I got her brush and asked Ben to help me hold her while I ran it through her long, beautiful blonde locks. He sat with me for several minutes, helping me make my wife beautiful for the orderlies who would come and take her away.

"I need to call Stephen," he said. "He'll help with the legal issues."

I hadn't even thought about that part of it, but it suddenly occurred to me that as her husband, I had to authorize the release of her body and a dozen other legal matters. And, I had to contact you two.

Obviously I didn't call you. As I was going through her things, looking for a phone number or address to contact you, I found the letter that she never mailed. The one you now have. It was then that I first thought she didn't want you to know about us. And it was because of that initial reaction that I had Stephen, Ben and Dr. Enzerillo, complete all the necessary paperwork, using her maiden name on all the forms. Stephen tried to talk me out of my decision. I wish now that I had listened to him. At that point I was confused and probably irrational. I felt that I was protecting her by keeping my existence and our relationship a secret – by fading into the scenery. I can't tell you how very sorry I am for that.

The rest of Jenna's story you know.

Ben took me to their house in San Francisco. He and Stephen put up with my incessant crying and depression for two weeks. They offered, as I said before, to let me stay there indefinitely. I think Ben wanted to make sure I wasn't infected and thought he would be able to convince me to get tested. Stephen tried to get me to draw again. They did everything they could to make me feel at home.

I went to the Fourth of July celebration with Ben and Stephen and a couple dozen of their other friends. We sat on a hill overlooking the Golden Gate Bridge and watched the fireworks. It rained that night. I sat all alone in the midst of a small crowd of people thinking of the totems that Jenna and I had between us. Bridges, rain, Laundromats, skinny dipping, Elvis, red dresses, black suits, deer, beer, friends…lots of friends. So many things remind me of her – so many every-day things. There is nowhere I can go without being reminded of her. But I knew that staying with Ben and Stephen was still too close to the pain.

I left quietly the next morning while Stephen and Ben slept. I greeted the sun on their front porch as I looked in all directions deciding which way would be best. I was going back on the road – back to the place Jenna had called my home. But my home was empty. There was nobody there to share the storms and the bridges. Nobody to laugh at my stupid jokes or make jokes for me to laugh at. Nobody to sing with. Nobody to dance with.

I left my friends a simple note.

Thank you for everything.
I'll be back sometime.
Tory

I haven't been back yet but I plan on it sometime, just like I said in the note.

With that, I think I'm going to end this letter. I've already taken a hefty piece of your time. I hope I've been able to fill in the gaps of those three weeks when you must have been so desperately worried.

It's been cathartic for me to get this out. Now I have to get up the guts to mail it.

I want to meet you some day. I really do want that. Perhaps I'll be passing through Pennsylvania and detour up to Mertztown. I hope I find you home.

Remember Jenna. I do.
Angus Tory McLeod

Interlude
Jenna

June something
Dearest folks,

How do I explain the past few days? I'm not even completely sure what day it is. This is going to be difficult because I'm crying so hard right now I can't see the paper. It doesn't help that I'm sitting in a Jeep outside a motel with only the light of the street lamp to show me what I'm writing. I know I have a lot of making up to do since my last letter but it seems I have so few words to describe what I'm experiencing. So few words but so much to tell you. I guess I should just get at it before I lose my nerve.

I remember telling you that I needed to find my white whale when I left home. Well…

THERE BE WHALES IN KANSAS!

I found it, or rather him. I found what I've been looking for.

It's a man! A beautiful, talented, unbelievable man. Who woulda thunk it?!

I thought I was looking for adventure, for experience and it turns out I was looking for love! Crazy! Madness! Me?

His name is Tory – at least that's what I call him. His full name is Angus Tory McLeod. Poor kid. But he wears it well. I can't imagine him being called anything else. He doesn't look like a Mike, or a Jim, or a Bill, or even a Rocco. I think my calling him Tory has changed his life. Who knew that could be so easy?

He's tall and thin and has the most angelic eyes. Dreamy eyes, mom would call them. I'm gushing. I shouldn't do that. It makes this sound like a teenage crush. It's much more than that and I should show more respect because it's my life now. Not to mention he's sleeping in the back seat and may be looking over my shoulder to see what I'm writing! (Just checked. He's not.)

How do I describe this man – this yin to my yang – this better part of me? He's my love – pure and simple. He's everything I could ever have expected in a soul mate. He's not rich in a monetary sense but he's the richest man I've ever known. (Tied with you, Daddy.)

He's a musician, a poet, an artist, a pauper, a pirate, a pawn and a king! (Ok, not a pirate.)

I'm getting silly.

He's a troubadour. He travels from town to town making his living with his guitar and his sketchbook. What better man could there be for me? He can't provide for my future but then I don't have much of a future anyway! Ok, bad joke. Now I'm crying again.

We've met some amazing people together. We're currently in Colorado with this wonderful couple. They let us sleep in their Jeep! They're taking us to Las Vegas with them. After that who knows where we'll go. We're kind of headed toward California but we haven't made that official yet.

More about Tory. He's really an amazing artist. He can draw just about anything and seems to be able to find the things that mean the most to people for the subject of his art. He's also a pretty good musician although I think his guitar has less time left on this earth than me. He's a little older than me. God this feels so stupid. I have to tell you about him but I can't find the words. ME! CAN'T FIND WORDS! You know it's gotta be love!

    I'm going to marry him. I just decided that.
    I'm going to marry him.
    I'm going to marry him.
    I miss you.
    I'll finish this tomorrow.

Continuation
Off the Road

Tory showed up on our back porch in the mid-Summer of that year. He had been wandering Eastern Canada and the Maritime states throughout the spring. He found himself on the New York-Pennsylvania border on the anniversary of their wedding in the Elvis Chapel, and felt compelled to come and visit us.

MaryBeth and I were in the kitchen. She was making lemonade. I was drinking it. We heard someone climb the creaky wooden steps on the back porch and then rap lightly on the door. MaryBeth answered it.

"I'm Tory," was the first thing we actually heard him say. Of all the times we had read the letter we had never imagined him looking or sounding the way he did. We had never heard his soft voice with its easy Southern drawl that fed the ears like warm biscuits smothered in butter. We had never pictured his finely sculpted face, too old for someone so young, too young for someone so old. And we had never seen the depth and the blueness of his magical eyes that opened like windows onto the ocean of a truly expansive soul.

He looked tired and hungry. He was about twenty pounds underweight for a man his size. He carried on his clothes and in his long sandy brown hair memories of a thousand miles of road. On his back was a threadbare rucksack, stitched together in places with fishing line, and slung over his shoulder, wrapped in plastic, was his faithful companion, Erik.

MaryBeth invited him in, which brought a smile to his eyes as well as his narrow mouth. He was afraid we might reject him. He unloaded his burden and set Erik gently by the door.

"He doesn't play anymore," he said, referring to the road-worn guitar. "I carry him with me anyway. He's a good listener."

The four of us sat in the kitchen until the sun went down.

MaryBeth asked questions. Tory answered them. Erik and I just listened, mostly. He told us where he had been since he wrote the letter and apologized on numerous occasions for "dealing with things so poorly."

I couldn't help but stare at the man. All this time I had been thinking of him as some sort of fictional character. I could never quite imagine he was real, but there he was in living color. And there was Erik, the trusty sidekick, and the rucksack that carried all of his worldly possessions including the omnipresent sketchpad and pencils. Around his neck was the chain that held the two silver and turquoise wedding bands. I stared at the smaller one, thinking about it wrapped around the ring finger of my little girl.

When darkness completely covered the hills he stood and said he should be going. He apologized again for all that had happened and for taking so much of our time. MaryBeth was up only a second before me. She insisted that he stay, as I was about to, and told him that his traveling days were over. He was going to stay with us. He tried to argue with her – such pride! I joined forces with MaryBeth and together we convinced him to stay, although he promised that it would only be for a short while.

His symptoms didn't show up until about a month after he arrived. We convinced him to see a doctor who confirmed the presence of the virus and the preliminary collapse of his immune system. Once again, MaryBeth and I were confronted with the prospect of losing a child to AIDS.

Tory took the news fairly evenly. At times it almost seemed like a relief to him that his time was short. He went regularly for treatments, which seemed to help for a while, but he had been exposed to so many different viruses and infections during his time on the road that we knew one of them would eventually come to claim him.

We spent a great deal of time talking about his travels, Tory and I. I took copious notes about the places he had been and the people he had met. He wrote down the lyrics to all of the songs he had written and recorded them all on tape for us, including *Three Weeks in June*. He drew sketches of the people he met, all from memory, which I included with my notes.

Every day we went out to the marker where we buried Jenna's ashes. I had the original marker removed that was inscribed with Jenna's maiden name, and replaced with an identical stone reading "Jennifer Baines McLeod." At Tory's request, the inscription included the words, "To wake, to touch you, tomorrow, soon."

Tory got sick in the late winter. His treatments kept him relatively stable, but some of the infections wreaked havoc on his system. He was bed ridden for weeks at a time periodically bouncing back, but never all the way. He preferred to stay at the house rather than "rot away in a hospital bed." We had a nurse come in each day to check his vitals and initiate any medical countermeasures he required.

On June 14, two years to the day after he and Jenna saw the deer in Sequoia National Park, Tory died. He must have sensed the end coming as he took the time to write a quick note and pin it to his pillow.

June 14, 1995
Dearest Mom and Dad,

I had another dream about Jenna last night. She was under the bridge in Kansas where we first made love. She was happy and healthy but extremely frustrated with me. She told me I was procrastinating.
"Hurry up, McLeod! Do you think I'm going to wait here forever?"
So, I'd better get going. You know how sarcastic she gets when she's agitated.
Thank you for everything – for your time and your patience, but especially your love.

Tory

Ending
Another Place to Begin

We had Tory cremated and buried his ashes alongside Jenna. We erected a second marker identical to Jenna's stating simply, "Angus Tory McLeod, A minstrel of a modern time."

I contacted Bernie and Denny in St. Louis, and Ben and Stephen in San Francisco, to tell them that Tory had died. Bernie and Denny were surprised to hear that Jenna had also passed. I asked if they would like to contribute the drawings Tory had made for them to a memorial showing of his work. Both couples not only offered the work, they offered their time to help arrange the event.

Ben and Stephen coordinated with Stephen's friend in San Jose to provide us a venue for the showing. The gallery was small enough to display the thirty or so sketches that Bernie was able to collect from the list of names Tory had given me. I hired a local musician to professionally record all of Tory's songs to be run as background music for the art show. Mixed between the songs were recitations of Tory's poems, recorded by the people for whom he had written them including an 82 year old woman from Atlanta who hired Tory to tend her garden for a two week stretch one summer.

Denny organized the party. She invited everyone on the list. We expected about half to actually show up but were both surprised and delighted when everyone came, with one exception. The only person missing from

Tory's list was Harlan Oster who passed away during the time Tory was writing us his long letter.

The event was an emotional roller coaster. Each person enthusiastically shared their stories about Tory alone, or Tory *and* Jenna, and listened carefully as others shared theirs. The walls of the gallery were lined with sketches of cars, dogs, motorcycles and a variety of people. The soundtrack played in the background as people mingled, some stopping to listen to a poem or a song that sounded familiar, some having their picture taken in front of the drawing Tory had done for them. And dear faithful Erik stood in his own glass display case with a small sign that read, "Erik. He's not much to look at but his voice is his beauty."

As the evening drew to a close, I gathered everybody in the small auction room of the gallery and called forward all of the people who were mentioned in Tory's letter. None of them had read or heard the letter, but I felt compelled to share it with them, as it is the one piece of work that was created by the man himself, and not the mysterious entity he called the Maestro. It was Tory's words that we would read, each person taking turns reading the part that involved him or her – from Dorlene to Ben. But it was MaryBeth who brought a hush to the crowd when she opened the notebook and read...

Dear Mom and Dad,
I know it must seem odd to receive a letter from a stranger with the above salutation. The truth is...

Fin

About the Author

David Telford was born a traveler who by the age of two had already journeyed more than 15,000 miles and visited a handful of countries. He captures his travels and interactions with the people he meets in his numerous poems, short stories, and full-length novels.

He makes his home in the suburbs of Chicago with his family and emotionally needy Rottweiler, but still sets out on adventures in other lands as often as he can.

This is his first publication.

Find out more about the author and his work at:

www.telfordbooks.com